Sophie and the New Girl

Other books in the growing Faithgirlz!™ library

The Faithgirlz!™ Bible
NIV Faithgirlz!™ Backpack Bible
My Faithgirlz!™ Journal

The Sophie Series

Sophie's World (Book One)
Sophie's Secret (Book Two)
Sophie Under Pressure (Book Three)
Sophie Steps Up (Book Four)
Sophie's First Dance (Book Five)
Sophie's Stormy Summer (Book Six)
Sophie's Friendship Fiasco (Book Seven)
Sophie Flakes Out (Book Nine)
Sophie Loves Jimmy (Book Ten)
Sophie's Drama (Book Eleven)
Sophie Gets Real (Book Twelve)

Nonfiction

Body Talk
Beauty Lab
Everybody Tells Me to Be Myself but I Don't Know Who I Am
Girl Politics

Check out www.faithgirlz.com

the beauty of believing

SOPHIE
and the New Girl

8

Previously titled Sophie Tracks a Thief

Nancy Rue

ZONDER**kidz**

ZONDERVAN.com/
AUTHORTRACKER
follow your favorite authors

We want to hear from you. Please send your comments
about this book to us in care of zreview@zondervan.com. Thank you.

ZONDERKIDZ

Sophie and the New Girl
Previously titled *Sophie Tracks a Thief*
Copyright © 2005, 2009 by Nancy Rue

This is a work of fiction. The characters, incidents, and dialogue are products of author's imagination and are not to be construed as real. Any resemblance to actual events or persons, living or
dead, is entirely coincidental.

Requests for information should be addressed to:

Zondervan, *Grand Rapids, Michigan* 49530

Library of Congress Cataloging-in-Publication Data

Rue, Nancy N.
   [Sophie tracks a thief]
   Sophie and the new girl / Nancy Rue.
     p. cm. (Sophie series ; [bk. 8]) (Faithgirlz!)
   Originally published in 2005 under the title, Sophie tracks a thief.
   Summary: As the Corn Flakes and other members of the Film Club work on a school
project about Cuban refugees in the 1980s, a newcomer's prejudices hurt Maggie and
challenge Sophie's ability to understand and practice Jesus' teachings.
     ISBN 978-0-310-71843-7 (softcover)
   [1. Prejudices—Fiction. 2. Cuban Americans—Fiction. 3. Friendship—Fiction. 4.
Imagination—Fiction. 5. Christian life—Fiction. 6. Family life—Virginia—Fiction. 7.
Virginia—Fiction.] I. Title.
PZ7.R88515Sjt 2005
[Fic]—dc22   2009004129

All Scripture quotations unless otherwise noted are taken from the *Holy Bible, New International
Version*®. NIV®. Copyright © 1973, 1978, 1984 by International Bible Society. Used by permission
of Zondervan. All rights reserved.

Any Internet addresses (websites, blogs, etc.) and telephone numbers printed in this book are
offered as a resource. They are not intended in any way to be or imply an endorsement by
Zondervan, nor does Zondervan vouch for the content of these sites and numbers for the life
of this book.

Published in association with the literary agency of Alive Communications, Inc., 7680 Goddard
Street, Suite 200, Colorado Springs, CO 80920. www.alivecommunucations.com

Zonderkidz is a trademark of Zondervan.

Interior art direction and design: Sarah Molegraaf
Cover illustrator: Steve James
Interior design and composition: Carlos Estrada and Sherri L. Hoffman

Printed in the United States of America

09 10 11 12 13 14 15 16 • 24 23 22 21 20 19 18 17 16 15 14 13 12 11 10 9 8 7 6 5 4 3 2 1

So we fix our eyes not on what is seen,
but on what is unseen.
For what is seen is temporary,
but what is unseen is eternal.

—2 CORINTHIANS 4:18

One

✿ 🐦 ❧

First we'll go to the cheerleaders' booth," said Sophie LaCroix's best friend, Fiona Bunting. The breeze loosened a strand of her golden-brown hair, and she tucked it behind her ear. "They've got corn dogs. And then we'll hit the Film Club—they're selling flan over there. And then we can stop off at the Round Table booth for kabobs—"

Sophie squinted at Fiona from behind her glasses while Fiona sucked in a breath. She hadn't taken one for a while.

"We're supposed to be filming the booths." Sophie nodded at the video camera in their friend Darbie O'Grady's hand. "Not pigging out at them."

Fiona grabbed a handful of candy corn from the chorus booth. "Who says we can't film and eat at the same time?"

Darbie O'Grady grinned, dark eyes dancing beneath her fringe of reddish bangs. "You're foostering about," she said. Although Darbie had lived in the United States long enough for her Irish accent to fade some, she still used her Northern Ireland expressions. So did Sophie.

"I guess I don't blame you for foostering," Sophie said. "Documentaries are boring."

"It's all about facts," Fiona said, her mouth stuffed.

"Facts aren't very creative." Sophie pushed her glasses upward on her nose. "I wish we were working on a *real* movie again."

"Uh-oh," Darbie said to Fiona. "She's got that look in her eye."

"You know it," Fiona said. Her own gray eyes were shining.

Sophie didn't need to see her brown ones to know what "look" they meant. She could feel it from the inside: that dreamy thing that happened when her mind started to wrap itself around a new character. If she still had her long hair, she would this very minute pull a strand of it under her nose like a mustache. That always helped her sort her thoughts. But it was impossible now that her hair was two inches high in fuzziness—although it was *long* compared to two months ago when she'd first shaved it off.

Sophie ran her hand over her fuzzy head. Closing her eyes, she saw herself as the tall, statuesque (that was one of Fiona's many impressive words) *Liberty Lawhead, swinging her briefcase as she marched briskly up the courthouse steps, heels clicking on the marble—*

"Hel-lo-o, So-o-phie." Darbie tugged playfully at Sophie's earlobe. "Miss Imes will eat the heads off us if we don't get *this* film done for Film Club."

"*Then* we'll tell her how we really want to do movies," Fiona said. "Corn Flakes Production–style."

Sophie nodded as she followed Fiona and Darbie and the smell of corn dogs across the field to the cheerleaders' booth. There Willoughby Wiley was practically doing a handspring waiting for them. "The Corn Flakes" was what the four of them, plus Maggie LaQuita and Kitty Munford, had called themselves ever since the Corn Pops, the popular girls in sixth grade last year, had told them they were "flakes."

That means we aren't afraid to be just who we are, the Corn Flakes had decided. So it only made sense that the movies they created from their amazingly intense daydreams were called Corn Flakes Productions.

But making a documentary about Great Marsh Middle School's Fall Festival for the new Film Club wasn't anything like making their own "flicks," as Darbie called them. Sophie sighed as she caught up to Darbie, who was already setting up the shot, and Fiona, who was already munching on a corn dog.

Willoughby's short mane of wavy, almost-dark hair trembled as she let out a shriek that always sounded to Sophie like a poodle yipping.

"Where have y'all been?" Willoughby said. "I've been waiting all day!" She waved her arms in what Sophie figured was a new cheerleading routine. She'd been to enough Corn Flake sleepovers to know Willoughby did cheers in her sleep.

"Be still, Willoughby," Darbie said. "Sophie has to interview you."

As Darbie started filming, Willoughby snatched up a corn dog in each hand and shook them like pom-poms. Two other cheerleaders posed beside her.

"What's the cheerleading booth up to?" Sophie said.

"We're selling corn dogs!" they all shouted together.

"Why?" Sophie said.

"Because they're good!" Willoughby said.

"No, eejit," Darbie said—using her Irish word for "idiot." "What are you going to use the money for?"

It's a good thing Mr. Stires has editing equipment back at school, Sophie thought. "To go to cheerleading camp this summer!" they all screamed.

"Thanks, girls," Fiona said, voice dry. "We'll call you if we can use you."

"Okay!" the squad cried out.

Willoughby's going to be great in our Liberty Lawhead film, Sophie thought. *She can lead the crowds of protesters in yelling … while the majestic Liberty Lawhead goes into battle for people whose rights are being tromped on. That was what made her a civil rights leader—*

"Beam yourself back down, Soph," Fiona said. "Let's hit the Film Club booth before all Senora's flan is gone."

Sophie pulled herself out of the 1960s, where she'd spent a lot of dream-time ever since they'd started studying the Civil Rights Movement in English/History block. When she got to the booth, Fiona was drooling over Senora LaQuita's shiny squares of sweet flan.

"I save you some, Fiona," the senora said. Maggie's mom was from Cuba, and Sophie loved her special way of speaking English.

Fiona pulled the plastic spoon out between her lips and closed her eyes. "It is *muy bueno,*" she said.

"That means 'very good,'" Maggie informed them. Maggie's words always fell like thuds, as if each one were a fact you couldn't argue with. With her steady dark eyes and solid squareness, the Corn Flakes usually *didn't* argue with her.

Right now Maggie nodded toward the camera, her black bob splashing against her cheeks. "Are you going to interview me?" she said. "I wish Kitty was here. She's better at this than me."

Kitty was the sixth Corn Flake, and Maggie's best friend. She had leukemia and was in the hospital in another town getting more chemotherapy, which, among other hard things, made her hair fall out. Sophie had shaved her head at the beginning of middle school so Kitty wouldn't be the only bald girl.

"I'm rolling," Darbie said.

"Tell us what the Film Club's up to here at the festival, Mags," Sophie said.

Maggie looked stiffly into the camera. "We're selling flan."

"What's flan?" Sophie said.

"It's like pudding."

There was a long pause. Fiona poked Sophie in the side.

"Have you sold a lot to make money for Film Club supplies?" Sophie said.

"We *did*," Maggie frowned, "until Colton Messik told everybody it was phlegm, not flan."

"What's 'phlegm'?" Sophie whispered to Fiona.

"Stuff you cough up when you have a cold," Fiona said.

"EWWWW!"

Darbie focused the camera on Miss Imes and their other sponsor, Mr. Stires. Miss Imes, their math teacher, pointed her dark arrow-eyebrows toward her short, almost-white hair. "Ready," Darbie said.

"Senora LaQuita has made some luscious *flan* for us," Miss Imes said into the camera. She didn't miss much, especially if it was some kid doing something wrong.

Sophie turned to their science teacher, Mr. Stires, who stood next to Miss Imes. He was short, bald, and cheerful, and his mustache stuck out like a toothbrush.

"Tell us about the equipment we're going to buy with the flan money," Sophie said.

Sophie heard Fiona groan as Mr. Stires launched into a lecture about DVD recorders.

"Oops, battery running low!" Darbie said after two very long minutes. "I'll get the extra one." She darted off.

"We could have been there for decades," Fiona said as she and Sophie followed. "Let's go for the kabobs."

11

Fiona took off for the Round Table booth on legs longer by several inches than tiny Sophie's, and Sophie hurried to keep up. Since Film Club had turned out to be pretty boring, being on the Round Table was Sophie's favorite school activity.

It was a special council of teachers and a few handpicked students who had set up an Honor Code for the school. They were responsible for deciding consequences for people who broke it, things that would help them learn to be better people instead of just punishing them.

No cases had been brought before them yet, and Sophie was anxious for one. It would be a great opportunity to be like Liberty Lawhead . . .

Who entered the room with her jaw set, looking down from her impressive height into the eyes of a heinous offender who had stomped on the rights of an innocent person. He looked back at her, his face set with stubborn heinous-ness, but she met his gaze firmly, without wavering. He finally dropped his eyes. He had obviously seen the honor in her face, honor he could never hope to match—

"What are *you* looking at?"

Sophie found herself blinking into an unfamiliar face. Hazel eyes, set close to a straight, very-there nose, blinked back at her. The girl shook sandy-blonde bangs away from her eyebrows and pulled back her upper lip. Sophie wasn't sure it was a smile, but she couldn't take her eyes off the gap between the girl's two front teeth.

"I said, what are you looking at?" the girl said.

"Nothing!" Sophie's high-pitched voice went into an extra-squeaky zone.

"You were looking at something if you were looking at me," the girl said. Sophie was sure she smiled then, although mostly it looked like she smelled something funny.

Fiona and Darbie joined them, Fiona giving Sophie a we-thought-you-were-right-behind-us look. "You're Phoebe, huh?" she said to the girl.

"Yeah. Phoebe Karnes. I just transferred into your PE class." Phoebe tossed her bangs out of her eyes again and licked her full lips. "I was in all the wrong classes—it was all messed up. What are y'all's names?"

As Fiona introduced everybody, Sophie studied Phoebe. She had a look Sophie hadn't seen on many girls in well-off Poquoson, Virginia: faded jeans a little tight and a little short, graying tennis shoes with untied laces, and a long-sleeved T-shirt with ANGEL printed on it in fading glitter. Earrings with rhinestones sparkling down the length of them dangled from her ears.

She's definitely not a Corn Pop, Sophie thought.

"So, if you're interviewing people, interview me," Phoebe said. She lifted her lip at the camera before Sophie could even think up a question. "Hi—I'm Phoebe! My opinion of the festival? It's hilarious. For instance, let me direct your attention to the arm-wrestling booth."

Phoebe pointed to several tables set against a display of neon-colored stuffed animals. Members of the GMMS eighth-grade football team were arm-wrestling kids for chartreuse elephants and hot-pink teddy bears.

"There goes another one down," Phoebe said to the camera. "Flop—right to the table like a wet noodle."

Sophie saw she was right. One after another, kids gripped a football player's hand and pushed until their faces turned purple and their arms slapped to the table.

"Get this one on film, Darbie," Fiona said.

Sophie felt a smile wisp across her face. Eddie Wornom, a more-than-just-chubby member of the heinous group of boys the Corn Flakes called Fruit Loops, was sitting down across from a fullback almost the size of Sophie's father.

Eddie glanced at B.J. Schneider, the Corn Pop standing behind him with her thumbs hooked into her hip-hugger pants. Behind her stood the other three Pops, all in ponchos that obviously didn't come from Wal-Mart, all with lip gloss shining.

"You better win this time, Eddie," Sophie heard B.J. say. Her pudgy cheeks were red, either from the crisp October air or because she was getting impatient with Eddie. He pushed so hard against the fullback's hand the veins in his neck bulged like ropes.

"If anybody can beat that football player, it's that bull Eddie," Darbie said from behind the camera.

"Nah, that's all blubber," Phoebe said. "See—there he goes!"

The eighth grader eased Eddie's arm to the table like he was knocking over one of the teddy bears.

"Eddie, you loser!" B.J. rolled her eyes with the rest of the Corn Pops.

"He cheated!" Eddie cried. "That—"

Sophie covered her ears so she wouldn't hear what came out of Eddie's mouth. It was usually gross.

"Hey, Jimmy! I bet you could win me a stuffed animal."

The Corn Flakes and Phoebe turned toward Julia Cummings, the tall leader of the Corn Pops. She was tilting her head at blond seventh grader Jimmy Wythe, so that her own dark auburn hair fell just so across her face. Jimmy looked as if he'd rather drown at the dunking booth than have Julia look at him that way.

"She should give up," Darbie whispered. "Sophie's the one he likes."

"He doesn't *like* me like me," Sophie said, voice squeaking. "*Eww.*"

It wasn't that Jimmy was at all heinous like a Fruit Loop. In fact, the Corn Flakes usually referred to him and his friends as Lucky Charms because they didn't make disgusting noises with their armpits or make fun of people until they withered. But Sophie just couldn't see wearing tons of makeup for one of them the way the Corn Pops did. Life was complicated enough.

"He's gonna do it!" Phoebe said.

Sophie stared as Jimmy shrugged and sat down across from the fullback.

"I give it fifteen seconds max," Phoebe said.

But Fiona shook her head. "Jimmy wins at, like, all these gymnastics competitions. That football player *wishes* he had Jimmy's arm muscles."

Darbie held the camera up just as Jimmy and the other guy linked hands. Immediately, both their faces turned red. The eighth grader got a concerned look in his eyes and grunted.

"He's fakin' it," Phoebe said.

But Jimmy didn't make a sound as he slowly pushed Mr. Fullback's arm flat onto the table.

"Dude," Phoebe said.

"I told you," Fiona said.

"I want the lime green one, Jimmy!" Julia said.

"We don't want *that* on film," Sophie said.

"That Eddie kid's about to explode." Phoebe's full lips spread into a smile. "I think it's funny."

"You stay and watch it, then," Fiona said. "Where to next, Soph?"

"Dunking booth," Sophie said.

She wanted to see Coach Nanini, the boys' coach she always thought of as Coach Virile because he actually *was* bigger than Sophie's dad. Besides, *virile* was such a masculine word. He was Sophie's favorite GMMS teacher.

"I'm taking you down, Coach!" Gill Cooper was yelling when they got there. Gill was one of the athletic girls the Corn Flakes referred to as Wheaties. She was about to pitch a softball at a target that, if she hit it, would dump Coach Nanini right into a huge vat of water.

"You couldn't hit the broad side of a barn!" Coach yelled back in his high-for-a-guy voice. To Sophie he looked like a big happy gorilla with no hair.

"Wanna bet?" Gill hurled the ball, and Coach Nanini went down with a splash that soaked everybody standing within two yards.

"Did you get it, Darbie?" Fiona said.

"In more ways than one," Darbie said. She rubbed the camera dry against her sweatshirt.

Suddenly a whole chorus of "Fight! Fight!" broke out, and it seemed like the entire festival crowd surged toward the snow-cone booth next to the dunking tank. Before she could turn around, Sophie was swept up by the mob, feet not even touching the ground. "Take him down, Eddie!" the kid directly next to her screamed. It was Colton Messik, the Fruit Loop with the stick-out ears.

Sophie swung her elbows around and got herself down onto the ground. Squeezing her eyes shut and digging her fingers in, she started to crawl.

"Hey, somebody get that girl out of the way!"

Sophie raised her head to see what girl they were talking about, but something came down hard on her back. She was flattened to the dirt.

16

Two

✿ ❋ ✺

"All right, break it up!" Coach Nanini's voice cut through the roar of the crowd, and whoever was on top of Sophie rolled off. She gasped for air.

"Good grief—are you all right, LaCroix?" Coach Yates, the girls' PE teacher, was suddenly beside her. Sophie couldn't mistake that voice either. It had yelled her name enough times in class.

But now Coach Yates was saying gently, "Let's make sure you're okay before you get up. Anything hurt so bad you can't move it?"

Sophie shook her head, cheek still in the dirt.

"I didn't even get to see who was goin' at it," some kid whined from the crowd.

"Eddie Wornom," somebody answered him. "He fell on that little seventh-grader chick."

"All right, everybody move on," Coach Nanini said. "Nothing to see here."

Sophie kept her head down until everybody shuffled away. If Eddie Wornom had been on her, she didn't want anybody seeing who she was. *Ewww.*

"He was fighting that gymnastics dude," the same kid said.

Gymnastics dude? Sophie thought. *Not Jimmy!*

Coach Yates told Sophie to try to sit up.

"Was it really Jimmy Wythe?" Sophie said as she struggled to get upright.

"Yes," Coach Yates said, "but he doesn't look as bad as you do."

"I'm okay."

"Except for the blood dripping from your nostrils and the scrape across your forehead."

Sophie rubbed her hand under her nose. Her fingers came away red.

By then the rest of the Corn Flakes had squatted around her. From the looks on their faces, Sophie was sure she was disfigured for life.

"No broken bones, though, I don't think," Coach Yates said. She shook her head, stirring the too-tight, graying ponytail that stuck out through the opening in the back of her GMMS ball cap. "You always end up at the wrong place at the wrong time, don't you, LaCroix?"

"Wherever Eddie Wornom is *is* the wrong place," Fiona muttered.

Sophie didn't remind her that it was against the Corn Flake Code to put people down, even when those same people took *them* down. She looked at her bloody fingers again. Literally took them down.

"Well, Sophie," said a voice behind them.

Sophie tilted her head back to look up at Mrs. Clayton, the head of the Round Table. She stood over them, frowning beneath her faded-blonde helmet of hair.

"Looks like we have our first case," she said. "Are you hurt?"

Sophie was suddenly tired of answering questions. She was starting to shake.

"Could somebody find my dad?" she said. "I want to go home."

Daddy was brought over from the pony rides, with Sophie's six-year-old brother, Zeke, screaming that he didn't get to ride long enough. After asking Sophie the same questions everybody else had, Daddy tucked her into the front seat of the pickup beside him, and they listened to Zeke wail all the way home.

"We didn't get to go to the bonfire! I didn't get to have a corn dog!"

"You ate two cotton candies and a taco." Daddy gave Sophie a sideways grin. "Your mother is going to be mad enough at me as it is."

"I wanna go to the bonfire!"

Only Daddy promising they would have their own fire in the backyard shut him up, which was good, since Sophie's head was starting to sting.

"Now, remember, Z-Boy," Daddy said as they pulled into the driveway, "don't upset Mama. I want you to chill."

Right, Sophie thought as Zeke ran to the house, still screaming about corn dogs. *Zeke doesn't know how to chill anymore.*

But Mama "chilled" him as nobody else could. With her arms around Sophie, she told Sophie's fourteen-year-old sister, Lacie, to get some hot dogs out of the freezer and dig out the cooking skewers. Then she described the wiener roast they'd have so well that Sophie could almost taste it. Zeke went happily outside with Daddy to pile on the wood.

"Now, Dream Girl," Mama said, turning Sophie around so she could inspect her face. "Where had you drifted off to when this happened?"

Mama smiled the wispy smile that Sophie knew matched her own. Everybody said she and Mama looked just alike, except that Mama actually *had* hair, and it was curly and high-lighted; she claimed it covered the gray that three kids had given her. And right now, Mama was puffier than usual. She was going to have a baby.

"I wasn't daydreaming this time," Sophie said. "Two boys were fighting, and I got caught in the crowd. Then Eddie Wornom fell on me—"

Mama's eyes got stormy. "They were fighting at the festival?"

"It was heinous," Sophie said.

"Let's get you cleaned up—come on."

Sophie sat in the chair by the window in her parents' upstairs bedroom while Mama cleaned the scrape on her forehead. Even though the hydrogen peroxide stung when Mama dabbed it on with a cotton ball, Sophie loved her alone time with her mom. It was a rare thing these days. When Mama wasn't resting, Zeke got most of her attention, acting out like he was practicing to be a Fruit Loop. Even now, Sophie could hear him hollering down in the yard.

"What's his deal?" Sophie said. "It's like he's Terrible Two all over again."

"He was never this bad when he was two." Mama blew softly on Sophie's forehead. "I hope this is just some phase he's going through. You girls never went through it."

"Girls are so much better than boys," Sophie said. "Do you hope our new baby is a girl?"

"I hope our new baby is healthy." Mama patted her tummy. "How do you feel about having a little brother or sister? We haven't had a chance to talk about it much."

Sophie hadn't had a chance to think about it much, either. Ever since the family meeting when Mama and Daddy had announced that there was going to be another LaCroix, Sophie had been wrapped up in Round Table and Film Club and Corn Flakes and Bible study with Dr. Peter and keeping her grades up so she could still have her video camera, according to her deal with Daddy. Besides, the new baby didn't seem real yet. Mostly it was just about Mama needing a lot of rest and Mama not getting upset and Mama taking vitamins the size of checkers.

Lacie came in then. She had a Daddy-look on her face, which wasn't hard because she, like Zeke, had his dark hair, his intense eyes, and his way of having everything figured out. "I hope you're almost done," she said, tossing her ponytail, "because Zeke is going to jump *into* the fire if we don't start cooking hot dogs in the next seven seconds." She grinned. "Which doesn't sound like a bad idea, actually."

"Lacie!" Mama said.

"Kidding—just kidding."

But as they followed Mama downstairs, Lacie looked at Sophie with a gleam in her eyes that clearly said, *"Which one of us is going to flush the kid down the toilet first?"*

The bonfire didn't go well.

At first, as Sophie smiled into the steam of her apple cider, she decided this was better than the bonfire at the festival. There were no Corn Pops or Fruit Loops doing stuff that would land them at the Round Table, where Liberty Lawhead would look at them solemnly and say . . .

"What were you thinking? Were you thinking that these innocents who are not as hot as you are, not as rich—do not have rights too? The right to walk down a hallway without being teased? The right to be exactly who they are without being told they are lame and weird?" *She leaned across the table, pointing her pencil in their direction—*

"Sophie," Daddy said, "I think that one's done enough."

"Oh, go all the way and burn it to a crisp, Soph," Lacie said.

Sophie looked at her black, shriveled hot dog.

Zeke, of course, wanted his charbroiled like that. When Daddy wouldn't let him, he pitched a fit that knocked his chair over into Mama's and sent them both tumbling to the ground.

Daddy yelled about Sophie not paying attention to what she was doing and Zeke and Mama almost falling into the fire, all the while dousing the flames with water as Zeke screamed. As Lacie and Sophie headed for the house with the skewers and the unopened bag of marshmallows, Lacie pointed out that they had been miles from getting burned.

"I thought it was the pregnant mother who was supposed to get cranky," Lacie said. "Not the pregnant father."

Behind them, Mama was saying, "I'm fine, honey," while Zeke howled about corn dogs and pony rides and everything else that had been denied him. Daddy was just howling—at everybody.

Sophie couldn't get to her room fast enough. She didn't even stop to examine the bandage on her forehead or the condition of the rest of her face. She just crawled under her pink comforter, within the sheer curtains Mama had hung around her bed, and pulled a purple pillow over her head.

"I hope you're there, Jesus," she whispered, "because I need to talk to you!"

That was what Dr. Peter—once her therapist and now her Bible study teacher—had taught her to do: to imagine Jesus and tell him anything she wanted and ask him anything she wanted. Since, according to the Corn Flakes, she was the best ever at imagining, she could see in her mind right now Jesus' kind eyes understanding absolutely everything.

This has been like the most confusing day, she said deep inside. *First that Phoebe girl hung out with us—and Jimmy Wythe got into a fight and I don't know how that's going to work out because he's on the Round Table Council and now he has to go in front of it—and I got trampled—and Mama asked how I felt about the new baby and I don't even know—then Zeke acted out like no other time—and then the worst: Daddy got all mad and yelled at everybody, even though it was only Zeke who was being evil. What's that about?*

She didn't expect an answer right then. Dr. Peter said that imagining Jesus talking back to her would be like putting words in his mouth. But she knew from experience that he *would* answer somehow, if she kept asking and kept waiting and kept looking in unexpected places.

Since that was the case, she made sure she was asking him exactly the thing she needed.

"Will you please help me find a way to make things more fair?" she whispered.

Then she added that she'd like for Zeke to please hush up so she could go to sleep—and then she did.

Three

By the time Sophie got to her locker before school on Monday, she'd heard three different rumors about what was going to happen that day.

"Eddie Wornom broke Jimmy Wythe's nose, and he's gonna get suspended by that Table thing."

"Jimmy Wythe knocked Eddie Wornom unconscious, and they're just gonna expel him, period."

"They broke Sophie LaCroix's back, and they're both being put in juvenile detention."

The fact that Sophie was standing right there, obviously in one piece, didn't change their minds.

"It's like there's nothing else to talk about," Darbie said to Sophie and Fiona at the lockers.

Fiona nodded toward the chattering knot of Corn Pops a few lockers down.

"I *know* Eddie didn't start it," B.J. was saying, cheeks already three shades of red. "He knows he can't play basketball if he gets in trouble."

Sophie knew what Fiona wanted to say: that Eddie was getting way too honkin' huge to run down a basketball court.

"That is just *wrong*, B.J.," Julia said. She raked her hand dramatically through her thick hair. "Jimmy obviously didn't start it. He's a lover, not a fighter."

Ewww, Sophie thought.

"I'll tell you one thing for sure," silky-blonde-haired Anne-Stuart said, sniffing juicily. The skinniest Corn Pop, she always seemed to have a sinus problem. "If that Round Table thing tries to suspend Eddie, the office won't let them. He's too valuable to the school."

"Do straighten them out, Sophie," Darbie said.

The four Corn Pops swiveled their heads at the same time and, as usual, looked at the Corn Flakes as if they had been invisible until then. Sophie had figured out that was the only way the Pops could express their attitude toward the Flakes—ever since the Flakes had exposed them and gotten them kicked off the cheerleading squad. The Pops would get suspended from school again if they did anything more than just pretend the Corn Flakes weren't there.

"Straighten us out on what?" said Cassie, the newest Corn Pop. Her more-blonde-than-red hair trailed in strings down her back, and her mouthful of blue braces were a perfect match for the Limited Too top hugging her ribs.

"Sophie knows about the Round Table," Fiona said. "She's on it."

Julia gave Sophie a bored look. "So?"

"So," Sophie said, straightening her tiny shoulders, "it's our job to sort out who did what and then help them behave better. We don't do punishments."

"Of course you don't." Anne-Stuart gave a particularly gooey sniff. "You can't. Like I said, Eddie's popular, and his father gives the school, like, a ton of money."

"It doesn't matter," Sophie said. "We just go by the Honor Code, no matter who the person is."

"Sounds lame to me," Cassie said.

B.J. gave her buttery-blonde bob an impatient shake. "You dis us all the time," she said to Sophie. "So how can you be fair to Eddie? You just better—"

"Shut up, B.J.," Julia said.

"Excuse me, girls." A wiry man with a tool belt was standing behind Darbie. His voice was sandpaper scratchy. "I need to work on that locker right there."

"Oh, sorry," Darbie said as she and Fiona and Sophie scooted out of his way.

The Corn Pops moved aside without looking at him.

I guess the janitor's invisible too, Sophie thought.

"What's wrong with it?" Fiona said.

"It's broken," B.J. said. "Duh."

"It's broken, all right," the janitor said. He ran his hand over his no-color hair that was so thin red scalp showed between the waves. "And it didn't happen by accident, far as I can tell."

Sophie liked his sandpaper voice. It was kind of grandfather-y, even though he didn't look as old, even, as Fiona's Boppa.

"That's Eddie's locker," B.J. said.

Julia looked into her until B.J.'s cheeks went pale.

"Well, it looks like Eddie was doing pull-ups on it," Mr. Janitor Man said, pulling a huge screwdriver out of the tool belt. "There are bars down in the gym for that. This wasn't made for it." He glanced over his shoulder without really looking at B.J. "You tell your friend Eddie that, would you?"

Sophie and the Corn Flakes escaped before Julia could stare B.J. into a dead faint.

When they got to their two-hour English/History block, Mrs. Clayton called Sophie to her desk right away. Her usually dry-looking face was almost glowing.

"Round Table will meet after school today with our two little warriors," she said. "Try not to listen to any of the scuttlebutt that's going around school between now and then."

Sophie was pretty sure "scuttlebutt" meant rumors.

Mrs. Clayton was nodding her blonde helmet of hair. "This will be our first opportunity to change some attitudes around here," she said. "Remember, it's not about taking sides. It's about making this a safe place for people to learn."

"What about Jimmy?" Sophie said. "Will he get kicked off the Round Table?"

"That's what we're going to decide," Mrs. Clayton said.

Liberty Lawhead walked solemnly to her desk in the Civil Rights for All office, feeling the weight of important work on her shoulders. As she slid into her chair, she saw the downtrodden she was about to save huddled in the waiting room. They looked so weary, so disappointed, and her heart ached for them. I will make change happen for them, she vowed. She doubled her fist and pounded it on the desktop—

"Did somebody knock?" Ms. Hess said.

Sophie swallowed as their other block teacher hurried her trim little self toward the door, gold hoop earrings bouncing. Oops.

Fiona cleared her throat then, the signal she used when Sophie drifted too far into a Sophie-World and lost track of what was going on in class. Sophie nodded at her and turned to the "I Have a Dream" speech she was supposed to be reading.

It's definitely time to start working on a Liberty Lawhead movie, she thought. *Before I get in trouble and lose the camera.* With the way Daddy was yelling again, it could happen even without her making less than a B.

The "scuttlebutt" had reached record heights by the time Sophie, Darbie, and Fiona met Maggie and Willoughby in the locker room for third-period PE.

Willoughby's eyes were practically the size of Frisbees as she pulled her GMMS T-shirt over her head. "Everybody says Jimmy started the fight," she said. "But he's so nice!"

"Whether he started it or not, I think he won," Fiona said. "He doesn't even look as banged-up as you do, Soph."

Sophie realized she hadn't even looked at Jimmy during first and second periods, or thought about the scrape across her very-exposed forehead. She'd been too caught up in Liberty Lawhead.

"Eddie has a bruise on his arm," Maggie said as she tied a neat knot in her shoelace and straightened up. "We better get out there, or we'll be late for roll call."

Maggie, Sophie thought as she followed her outside, had never been late for anything in her life. If there was a rule, Maggie would follow it. Gill gave Sophie a soft punch on the arm as they lined up. "Hey, Sophie," she said, "is that Round Table like a court where you decide who's guilty and stuff?"

Before Sophie could answer, another voice poked itself in.

"I already know who's guilty," said Phoebe. "I saw the whole thing."

"Of course you did," Fiona said. She grinned at Sophie.

"So what happened?" Gill said.

She and her friend Harley, and the twin Wheaties, Nikki and Vette, gathered with the Corn Flakes around Phoebe, whose eyes took on a sharp gleam. She gave everybody that sort-of-a-smile Sophie remembered from the festival. Sophie zeroed in once again on the gap between Phoebe's front teeth. Big teeth, Sophie noted.

"The chubby kid couldn't stand it when Gymnastics Boy won that retarded stuffed animal for Little Miss Don't You

Think I'm Cute," Phoebe said. "So he follows him around, working himself into a sweat."

Phoebe pushed up her sweatshirt sleeves and lowered her head like a bull. Her nostrils were actually flaring. Willoughby gave her poodle shriek.

"Finally," Phoebe went on with the group around her watching, mouths open, "Chubbo can't stand it any longer, and he goes up to Gymnastics Boy. He doesn't even say anything, he just shoves him—"

Phoebe stepped forward with her hands outstretched and shoved Maggie backward at the shoulders. A shrill whistle shattered the moment, and Coach Yates was suddenly on them.

"What's this about?" she yelled.

"I was demonstrating," Phoebe said. Her eyes were still on Maggie.

"If demonstrating means you have to put your hands on somebody, Karnes, you can't do it. Period." Before Sophie could get her hands over her ears, Coach Yates put her whistle to her lips and gave it an extra-long blow. "All right, let's hit the volleyball court!"

The Wheaties took off. Phoebe motioned the Corn Flakes toward her. "Since she interrupted, let me just cut to the chase," she said. "Gymnastics Boy defended himself, but he should have taken Chubbo out totally, in my opinion." She looked straight at Maggie. "I bet you thought the same thing."

Maggie blinked. "I wasn't even there."

"Well, I'm just saying. You people like a good fight, right?"

"Who wants detention over here?" Coach Yates yelled.

Everybody scattered for the court, except for Fiona, who held on to Sophie's sweatshirt as they ran. "What did she mean, 'you people'? Not us!"

"I don't know," Sophie said. "Mrs. Clayton told me I'm not supposed to be listening to rumors anyway."

"Then we better stay away from that Phoebe girl," Fiona said. She put her hand up. "I know, I know, we still have to be decent to her. Corn Flake Code. But decent doesn't mean we have to be her best friend."

"I'm *fine* with that," Sophie said. Because Phoebe Karnes made her feel more than a little bit squirmy inside.

During lunch that day, the Corn Flakes met in Mr. Stires' science lab to edit the Fall Festival film. Since only two people could use the equipment at the same time, Fiona and Maggie took that over while Darbie filmed Sophie doing an introduction. Willoughby "directed," which meant she stood behind Darbie doing cheer motions. Sophie was starting her introduction over for the third time when Fiona let out a *"Score!"*

"You guys have to see this!" she said. "Come here—quick!"

All of them, including Mr. Stires, hurried over to her and Maggie.

"Whatcha got?" Mr. Stires said.

"Only the proof of who started the fight." Fiona shoved the stubborn strand of hair behind her ear and pointed to the screen. "Look."

"Coach Nanini getting dunked," Darbie said.

"No, look behind him, at the snow-cone booth." Fiona ran the film back and played it in slow motion. "Watch what's happening."

Sophie squinted through her glasses. "Hey!" she said. "That's Eddie—shoving Jimmy!"

"Just like that one girl told us," Willoughby said. "He *did* start it!" She punctuated her words with a poodle shriek.

Sophie watched, smile spreading. In the background of the dunking footage, Jimmy took a step backward, shaking his head. Eddie kept moving toward him. Just as Eddie threw the first punch and Jimmy ducked, there was a splash of water, and the film stopped.

"It looks like you just made Sophie's work at the Round Table a piece of cake, girls," Mr. Stires said. Even his bald head was shining. "Let's polish this up for prime-time viewing."

"Ladies and Gentlemen of the Round Table Council," Sophie said that afternoon in her best Liberty Lawhead voice, "I have not shown you this film to prove who is guilty, but to show who needs help. I have a dream that we can change Eddie Wornom's attitude, and the attitude of every other student who needs it. Thank you."

There was a murmur of agreement as Sophie took her seat. Jimmy gave Sophie a shaky smile. Across the table, Mrs. Clayton nodded. Sophie was pretty sure she hadn't missed the "I Have a Dream" part.

But I was being sincere, Sophie thought. After all, Liberty Lawhead never used the words of people like Dr. Martin Luther King Jr. simply to impress people.

Liberty folded her hands neatly on the table. She didn't have to try to impress people. She merely did her job and did it well. At this very moment, she was about to change the life of the angry young man who couldn't keep his fists to himself. She tilted her face toward the head of Civil Rights for All, Mr. Virile—

"I suggest," Coach Nanini was saying, "that we use our Campus Commission program with Eddie."

The eighth-grade girl on the council, a serious brunette named Hannah who wore contact lenses that made her blink a lot, raised her hand. "Is that like community service, only they do it at school?"

"Yard duty," said the eighth-grade boy with the two pimples on his chin.

"He'll have work to do on campus during lunch and after school," Coach Nanini said, "but I'm going to use that time to work on anger management with him."

Pimple Boy grinned, showing the rubber bands on his braces. "So he'll think he's picking up trash, but he's really getting therapy."

"Thank you, Oliver," Mrs. Clayton said drily. "We can always count on you to sum things up for us."

News that the Film Club's footage had brought Eddie down spread like a rash of poison ivy the next day. No matter how many times Sophie explained that bringing people down wasn't the Round Table's goal, nobody believed it. Least of all Eddie.

During announcements first period, Miss Imes got on the intercom in the office and said that Film Club was meeting during lunch, and new members were welcome to join. When the Corn Flakes got to third-period PE, Willoughby's eyes were once more Frisbee-size.

"Before Miss Imes even got done with the announcement," she said, "Eddie goes, 'Film Club is a bunch of losers. All they do is try to get stuff on people and turn 'em in.'"

"Well," Fiona said cheerfully, "at least we don't have to worry about Eddie joining Film Club."

Sophie sighed. "I don't think *anybody* will want to join Film Club unless we make it more exciting."

But somebody else did want to join. When the Corn Flakes showed up in Mr. Stires' room that day at lunch, there sat Phoebe. Gap-toothed smile and all.

Four

❀ 🕊 ❋

Welcome to Film Club," Miss Imes said to Phoebe. "And you are?"

"Phoebe Karnes, and I have a *ton* of acting experience."

Miss Imes twitched an arrow-eyebrow. "We aren't so much about acting as we are about the art of film, the technical side."

Fiona raised her hand. "Uh, Miss Imes?"

"Yes, Fiona," Miss Imes said in her voice-as-pointy-as-her-eyebrows.

Fiona gave Sophie a poke.

"We wanted to talk to you about that," Sophie said. "We really want to act in our films. We can show you what we mean."

"Do you have the films, Mags?" Darbie said.

Maggie, of course, produced the Corn Flakes Productions' Treasure Book and opened it to the back, where all their DVDs were neatly tucked into plastic sleeves.

"These are some of the movies we've made," Sophie said.

Miss Imes' other eyebrow went up, and Mr. Stires stroked his mustache. It didn't look good.

"So pop one in." Phoebe shook her bangs out of her eyes. "Let's see what ya got."

Maggie slipped a DVD into the player, and the title *Medieval Maidens* glowed on the screen in the gold letters Kitty had

33

designed before she left for the hospital. The sight of them made Sophie sad.

But it was hard to stay that way watching herself and the other Corn Flakes cavort across the screen in the flowing gowns and pointy hats, and at times shiny armor, which Senora LaQuita and Maggie had made. It *was* hard to hear what their characters were saying, though, because Phoebe talked through the entire thing.

"Costumes aren't bad," she said.

"Dude—who taught you guys swordplay?"

"Oops, somebody dropped a line there—nice save, though."

"Yeah, get them with that speech, Sophie Baby. That's the best piece of acting in the whole thing. You're cookin'—you're hot."

Sophie didn't know whether to tell Phoebe to shush or keep it up. She was giving Corn Flakes Productions great reviews—sort of.

When Kitty's THE END appeared, both Mr. Stires and Miss Imes clapped. Phoebe whistled through her teeth. Sophie wondered if that space between them helped her do that.

"All right, I see the potential," Miss Imes said. "Go ahead and introduce drama. But we still expect you to continue to improve your technical skills."

"I don't know about technical stuff," Phoebe said, shrugging. "But trust me, I can act."

"I don't doubt it for a moment," Miss Imes said.

Fiona watched Phoebe exit, leaving a trail of acting credits behind her. "I said we'd be decent to her, but I didn't know we'd have to work with her."

"Maybe it won't be that hard." Willoughby's bubbly voice flattened. "You think?"

Darbie fiddled with her bangs. "She's different—and we're all about accepting people being different—"

Her voice trailed off. There was a big question mark in the air. They all looked at Sophie.

"She's just not different the way we're different," Sophie said. "She's like, way bossy—"

"She thinks she's ready for Hollywood," Fiona said.

Willoughby's little eyebrows knitted together. "It's like, she could be mean if she didn't like somebody."

"She doesn't like *me*," Maggie said. Her words fell harder than usual.

"Really, Mags?" Darbie said. "You mean, because she pushed you when she was talking about the fight?"

"She said she was just demonstrating," Willoughby said.

So far, Sophie couldn't see anything in Maggie's face.

"I'm just saying she doesn't like me," Maggie said.

"Which means it won't be that much fun for you," Fiona said. "I say we—"

"We can't 'say' anything," Sophie said. "This isn't Corn Flakes Productions, it's the Film Club. We don't get to say who can and can't be in it."

Willoughby seemed to wilt. "Then what do we do? Quit?"

"No way!" Fiona said.

"Then what, Sophie?" Darbie said.

Sophie nodded slowly. "The only thing we *can* do. We talk to Dr. Peter."

Fortunately, there was no Film Club meeting the next afternoon, the day they always met Dr. Peter at the church for Bible study. It was a good thing his class was based on the problems they brought in, because they hauled in a big one that day.

Dr. Peter was waiting for them with an eye-twinkly smile on his face. Their different-colored beanbag chairs and matching Bible covers formed a circle.

Sophie loved Dr. Peter more than any grown-up outside her own family. He was the one who had taught her to make films from her daydreams instead of escaping into them and missing what was going on in real life. Now that he led their Bible study, he taught cool things like that to the whole group. That included all the Corn Flakes except Willoughby, who had cheerleading practice after school, plus two of the Wheaties, Harley and Gill.

"You girls look like you're ready to pop open like a soda can." Dr. Peter grinned at them in that way that made his short, gelled curls seem to perk right up. It was impossible not to feel like everything could be okay with Dr. Peter around. "Let the fizzing begin," he said.

"Well, there's this girl," Fiona said.

She plunged into the story of Phoebe, with Darbie and Sophie adding details. The Wheaties put in a few of their own.

"I didn't like the way she pushed Maggie," Gill said.

"Did that bother *you*, Maggie?" Dr. Peter's eyes looked concerned.

Maggie shrugged. "She was just telling a story, I guess."

"She needs to lighten up," Gill said. "Only we're not supposed to put her down, are we?"

"We're just supposed to try to help people be better, right?" Sophie said.

Dr. Peter grinned at them again. "What do you need me for? You already know the answers."

"But what if I don't like those answers?" Fiona said. "This isn't very Christian, but I don't especially want to help her. She's just sort of—"

"Okay, tell you what," Dr. Peter said. "Let's dig into a Bible story and see if we can't figure this out."

"That's class, Dr. Peter," Darbie said.

Sophie liked it when Darbie said that, especially about Dr. Peter. He *was* great.

He had them turn to the Gospel of Luke, chapter 15, verse 1. They were all getting pretty good at finding their way around in the Bible, and everybody found it in the New Testament right away. Sophie prepared to go into imagination mode. "I want you to picture yourself as one of the 'bad guys' this time," Dr. Peter said.

"I don't want to be a bad guy," Maggie said.

"Nobody does," Dr. Peter said.

Fiona grunted. "I know some people that do. Oops, sorry, Dr. P. Go on."

"Trust me, you'll understand it better if you put yourself in the place of one of the teachers of the law."

"Those blackguards who were always blathering to Jesus about following the rules?" Darbie said.

She pronounced "blackguards" like "blaggards," one of Sophie's favorite Darbie-words. Sophie pressed her lips into a tight line and made her body stiff, so she'd feel more like a blackguard who couldn't even smile because having fun was against the rules.

"Now imagine that you are there," Dr. Peter said in his soft about-to-read voice. "And Jesus is talking to you."

Sophie pictured an outside hallway with columns, like she'd seen in Bible story books. With imaginary sandals on her feet and the taste of Israel dust on her tongue, she was ready.

"'Now the tax collectors and "sinners" were all gathering around to hear him,'" Dr. Peter read. "'But the Pharisees and the teachers of the law—'" He paused. "That's you."

"Got it," Fiona said.

"'The teachers of the law muttered, "This man welcomes sinners and eats with them."'"

Sophie pinched her Pharisee face tighter. *How wretched*, Sophie/the Pharisee thought. *Those slime.*

"'Then Jesus told them this parable—'"

"What's a parable?" Maggie said.

Sometimes it was hard to stay in character with Maggie there. She wasn't the Corn Flake with the most imagination.

"A parable is a story that's told to teach a lesson," Dr. Peter said. Sophie could hear the grin in his voice. "Like this one is about to do, any minute now."

Sophie tightened back into her Pharisee self.

"This is Jesus talking now. 'Suppose one of you has a hundred sheep and loses one of them. Does he not leave the ninety-nine in the open country and go after the lost sheep until he finds it?'"

Of course, Sophie/the Pharisee thought. *It doesn't take a brain surgeon to figure that out.* She knew they didn't have brain surgeons in Bible times, but it was the best sarcastic thing she could think of on short notice.

"'And when he finds it,'" Dr. Peter read on in his Jesus-voice, "'he joyfully puts it on his shoulders and goes home. Then he calls his friends and neighbors together and says, "Rejoice with me; I have found my lost sheep."'" *Get to the point, man*, Sophie/the Pharisee thought. *I'm an important person. I can't stand around here all day listening to stories. She/he tugged impatiently at his long beard.*

"'I tell you that in the same way there will be more rejoicing in heaven over one sinner who repents than over ninety-nine righteous persons who do not need to repent.'"

Maggie said, "What does 'repent' mean exactly?"

So much for imagining. Sophie wasn't enjoying being a bad guy to Jesus anyway.

"'Repent' means you admit that you've messed up," Dr. Peter said, "and you accept the forgiveness of God that's always there for you. Then you change your life."

Fiona leaned back in her purple seat, crackling the beans. "No offense," she said, "but what's this got to do with Phoebe? Are we supposed to try to save her, like, get her to be—what was that—'righteous,' instead of a sinner?"

"God is the only one who can save her," Dr. Peter said. "Matter of fact, he's the only one who can change her at all."

"So what do we do?" Maggie held a gel pen, like she was ready to write down his answer.

Dr. Peter pushed his glasses up by wrinkling his nose. "For starters, you can pray for her and appreciate her, the way Jesus does a lost sheep. Do that instead of putting her down. Jesus will go after her. God loves her just as much as he loves you." He rubbed his hands together. "There's more to this story, but let's just concentrate on that for right now."

"That sounds pretty easy," Fiona said. "We can do that, right?"

Everybody nodded, although Maggie didn't look all that enthusiastic to Sophie. "I'm staying away from her," Maggie said.

"Don't quit the Film Club, Mags!" Darbie said.

"I won't," Maggie said. "I'll just stay away from her."

"As long as you're praying, Maggie," Dr. Peter said. "Just remember that we all get lost now and then."

Sophie rested her chin on the edge of the Bible. Phoebe was lost? She didn't act that lost. She acted like she knew everything.

But if the great civil rights leader Dr. Barton Gunther Prince Jr. says we must pray for her, then we must, Liberty Lawhead thought.

But as a civil rights leader herself, she must do more than pray for this actress, Diva Dramatica. If only she knew what.

"Sophie-Lophie-Loodle."

Sophie's eyes popped open to see Dr. Peter's eyes twinkling at her.

"Your dad's here to pick you up," he said. "Who were you?"

"Liberty Lawhead, civil rights leader," Sophie said.

"A noble profession." Dr. Peter's eyes twinkled some more. "I can't wait to see this film."

Daddy was in the truck waiting for her, and Lacie was with him.

"I wanted to talk to both of you without Zeke around," he said as Sophie climbed into the backseat of the crew cab.

Lacie gave a grunt. "It was either take a ride in the truck or lock the kid in the closet."

In the rearview mirror, Sophie saw a trace of a smile go through Daddy's eyes.

But by the time they got home, Sophie wasn't smiling, and Lacie looked like she wanted to smack somebody.

Because Daddy announced that he'd be out of town the next week, and they needed to help Mama with Zeke after school. Even their protests that they had stuff to *do* after school didn't sway him. The "game plan," as Daddy put it, was that Lacie had Zeke duty Monday and Wednesday, and Sophie had it Tuesday and Thursday.

"With a new baby coming, we'll all have to take a hit for the team," Daddy said. "Just keep him out of your mother's hair for a couple of hours while she fixes dinner and gets some rest. No big deal."

Uh-huh, Sophie thought as she nodded at him. The former Zeke was no big deal. The little Act-Out King he'd become was the biggest deal in family history. And what about her busy schedule? Especially her making-a-film-about-Liberty-Lawhead time?

That night, Sophie imagined Jesus the minute she crawled under the covers. His kind eyes were there as she asked him first to deliver her from this evil, and then she gave in and asked him to help her want to do this for Mama. As she drifted off to sleep, she half dreamed of Jesus running after Zeke—but it was tough to imagine her screaming little brother as a lost lamb.

Five

When Sophie got to first period the next morning, Ms. Hess was writing on the board: CIVIL RIGHTS GROUP PROJECT.

Everything in Sophie snapped to attention. She was sure even her spiky hair stood up straighter. *Project* was one of her favorite words. So was *group*, if that meant the Corn Flakes could work together. And, of course, she was all about *civil rights* now. Could this *get* any more perfect?

It could, and it did.

"Divide into groups of your own choosing," Ms. Hess said when class started. Her lips pronounced each word precisely, which Sophie wished she could do. It would make her sound more like Liberty Lawhead.

"Your groups may include people from the other section," Ms. Hess went on, "since you will do the work for this project outside of class."

Sophie covered her mouth so she wouldn't squeal out loud. From two rows over, Fiona was mouthing all the Corn Flakes' names to her.

Mrs. Clayton put her palm up to stop the buzz. "We want your group to ponder this question: How did the Civil Rights

Movement of the 1960s affect the way people have respected the rights of minorities since then?"

Julia's hand shot up, and she smiled syrupy-sweetly at Ms. Hess. Sophie knew that was part of the Pops' plan to get back on Ms. Hess's good side, since she was the cheerleading adviser who had kicked them off the squad.

"I thought," Julia said, dripping a smile, "that after the law changed, everybody was equal and civil rights wasn't a thing anymore."

"It most certainly is still a 'thing,'" Mrs. Clayton said. "Racial prejudice has always been present in American society, and it continues to be." She drew two long, wavy lines on the board. "The idea that all people are equal is the main flow that has shaped our country and how we live." Mrs. Clayton drew some hard, straight lines moving in the opposite direction from the flowing ones. "As long as there are people who think some races are inferior to others, that will run against what this nation stands for, and some people won't get fair treatment in jobs, things like that." She tilted her helmet head toward them. "Your task is to take one of the research areas from the list Ms. Hess is handing out and decide whether what the great civil rights leaders of the 1960s did has actually helped in that area to stop this current of prejudice." She pointed to the hard lines.

"How long does our report have to be?" Anne-Stuart said.

"No written reports," Mrs. Clayton said. "We want you to make a creative presentation to the combined two classes to show what you find out."

All through PE Darbie, Sophie, and Fiona told Maggie and Willoughby about the project assignment. They decided that whatever topic they picked, they'd do a film—and maybe it could be their next Film Club movie too. Mr. Stires had such awesome equipment.

"Pinky promise," Darbie said when they were closing up their gym lockers. "We're going to make the most class film ever."

Each girl hooked her little fingers and linked them with the Corn Flake's on each side of her until they were connected in a circle.

"What's going on?" said someone outside the circle.

Sophie felt Fiona's pinky tighten on hers. "Hi, Phoebe," Sophie said. "We're just—um—doing our friend thing."

"Cool." Phoebe shook her bangs out of her eyes. "That would make a good bit in one of our movies. See y'all at lunch."

"She's eating with us?" Willoughby said after Phoebe left.

"We have Film Club at lunch," Maggie said, words thudding.

Sophie felt another *uh-oh* coming on.

Phoebe wasn't the only other person who showed up for Film Club after fourth period. Jimmy Wythe and two of his friends, Nathan and Vincent, were there too. At least, Sophie thought, they were all Lucky Charms. If a Fruit Loop or a Corn Pop had shown up, she might have given up film directing forever.

"How's this gonna work for our project with all these people?" Fiona whispered to Sophie.

"Fiona," Miss Imes said, pointing her eyebrows, "do you want to share with the whole group?"

Fiona stuck out her bag of sour cream and onion chips. "Anybody want some?"

"Me," Phoebe said, and took the whole bag.

"That isn't what I was referring to," Miss Imes said.

All the Corn Flakes looked at Sophie, and Miss Imes tucked in her chin. "Is there a problem?"

The Corn Flakes looked at Sophie again.

"What?" Phoebe said.

"I think they want you to speak for them, Sophie," Mr. Stires said with a chuckle.

Trying to pronounce carefully the way Ms. Hess did, Sophie explained about the project. "The problem is," she said, even more carefully, "not everybody in the club is in our project group."

"We could be, since we're in the block too." Jimmy's bright blue eyes seemed shy as he glanced at Sophie. "I figure since you helped me prove I didn't start that fight, we could—y'know—sorta help you."

Nathan nodded his curly head. Vincent just watched everybody out of his very thin face. He always looked very scientific to Sophie, like somebody on a *Star Trek* rerun.

"We're gonna need guys," Phoebe said. "I can play a boy—I can play anything—but why waste me on that when we can get actual males?" She poked her finger toward Vincent. "Can you act?"

"Yeah." Vincent looked at her poking finger like it was a fascinating insect. "We all can."

Nathan turned scarlet all the way up to the tips of his ears. He didn't usually say much, Sophie remembered. He just communicated by the shade of red on his face.

By now, Fiona was clearing her throat so hard Sophie thought she was going to cough up a hair ball.

"Do you have a problem with that, Fiona?" Miss Imes said.

"Phoebe's not in either one of the English/History blocks," Fiona said.

Miss Imes' eyebrows almost disappeared into her hair. "And your point is?"

"I get it," Phoebe said.

Sophie squirmed and held her breath.

"You guys think if I don't have to do the movie for a class I might, like, drop out or something and you'd end up getting a bad grade. I'd think that too if I was you — but y'all don't know me." Phoebe gave her bangs a dramatic toss. "When it comes to acting, I am, like, obsessed. I wouldn't walk out on a play or something if I was *dying*. You'll get an even better grade on this project because I'm in it — trust me."

"You certainly don't have any confidence issues," Miss Imes said.

Mr. Stires chuckled, but Sophie didn't see anything funny. Phoebe had just pushed herself into the Corn Flakes' special project, and the teachers had let her.

Nathan and Vincent looked at Jimmy, who scratched his blond head and shrugged his big-for-a-seventh-grader's shoulders.

"Works for me," he said.

Sophie could see *It doesn't work for us!* in every one of the Corn Flakes' eyes, except for Maggie. Her eyes had no more expression than a pair of pebbles.

"What wouldn't work for us," Miss Imes said, "is your using Film Club time and equipment to work on a class project that can't include everyone in the club. I'll go talk to Ms. Hess and Mrs. Clayton right now to make sure Phoebe can be involved. Otherwise, no deal."

After she left the room, Mr. Stires said, "I think it will work out. Go ahead and pick your topic, and I'll be right over here." Then he escaped into the lab.

"Sweet!" Phoebe said. "This is going to be cool. What are our choices? Let's see that sheet."

She snatched Darbie's list out of her hand.

Darbie snatched it back. "I'll read it out loud," she said.

Sophie groaned inside. How were they supposed to pray for this bossy girl, much less "appreciate" her? *"God loves her just as much as he loves you,*" Dr. Peter had said. Sophie was glad *God* did—

Darbie read the list, but nothing on it seemed to shout, "Take me! Take me!" Sophie tried to think what Liberty Lawhead would want to get into.

" 'Discrimination against Latinos,' " Darbie read. She looked up. "What's a Latino?"

Phoebe poked the usual finger toward Maggie. "Like her. Mexican."

"I'm Cuban," Maggie said.

"Same thing. You all speak Spanish." Phoebe tapped Darbie's sheet. "Go on."

"Wait a minute," Vincent said. A big, loose grin filled up most of his face. "We could do that one—y'know, since Maggie's a Latino person."

Sophie looked nervously at Maggie. She was sitting very still.

"Do you care if we do that, Mags?" Fiona said.

Maggie shrugged.

"We did a film about me being Irish," Darbie said. "The Corn—well, people stopped teasing me after that."

"Nobody teases Maggie about being Cuban, though," Sophie said.

Willoughby gave a half-shriek. "I never even knew she *was* Cuban until I met her mom."

"Her mom's cool," Jimmy said.

"She made that phlegm stuff," Vincent said.

"Flan!" the Corn Flakes said in unison.

Vincent blinked. "It was good. Anyway, if Maggie's okay with it—"

"Would everybody stop talking about me like I'm not here?"

Sophie glanced at Maggie. Her dark eyes finally had expression. They were flashing.

"Sorry, Mags," Fiona said. "Just tell us if you want to do it, yes or no."

"I vote no," Phoebe said.

"Is your name 'Mags'?" Fiona said. Sophie could tell Fiona was gritting her molars.

"Just listen," Phoebe said.

Do we have a choice? Sophie thought.

"I don't see how we're going to do a movie about Cubans getting their civil rights violated if we only have one Cuban in the group." She panned the circle with her eyes. "I'm sure not gonna play a Cuban."

"You have the wrong color hair anyway," Willoughby said. She gave a random shriek.

"Some Cubans have light hair," Maggie said.

"I never saw one." Phoebe pushed her finger into the gap between her teeth.

"How would you know?" Vincent said in his scientific voice. "You thought she was a Mexican."

"I want to do it."

Sophie stared at Maggie.

"You sure, Mags?" Darbie said.

"We don't have to," Fiona said. "There's other stuff on the list."

Willoughby flung an arm around Maggie's neck. "We know you don't like to be the main character—"

"What, are all of you her mother or something?" Phoebe pointed her finger yet again at Maggie. "Do you want to do it or not?"

"I said I do," Maggie said. "And they aren't my mother. They're my friends."

Phoebe shrugged. "That's cool. Okay—I'll play somebody who stages a protest march or something. I'm good in parts where I get in people's faces and yell."

"We don't even know if there's going to be a part like that," Fiona said. Sophie could tell her teeth were practically cemented together by now. "We do the research first. That's usually my job."

"I'll help you," Vincent said.

"Then we work out the script by playing with scenes. Maggie writes it down—"

"I can put it on my computer," Nathan said. They were the first words he'd uttered the whole time. His face was the shade of a tomato.

"Then we cast the roles," Fiona went on. "And the only one we know right now is Sophie's."

"Liberty Lawhead," Sophie said. "Civil rights leader."

"Don't we get to audition for that?" Phoebe said.

"No!" everybody said. Including Jimmy and Vincent.

Phoebe's eyes went round. "Okay," she said. "Don't have a heart attack. But just so you know: that's not the way it's done professionally."

"That's the way it's done here," Fiona said.

There was a stiff silence. Sophie tried not to take big mad-breaths that everybody would hear.

"Works for me," Jimmy said finally.

If he hadn't been a boy, Sophie would have hugged him.

Six

✿ ⌂ ❀

Miss Imes came back to tell them that Ms. Hess and Mrs. Clayton said Phoebe could be involved in the project.

"As long as the rest of you do all the research," she said. "I personally think Phoebe will add a great deal to the film."

Sophie felt prickles on the back of her neck.

Phoebe threw out both skinny arms. "Fabulous! I'm gonna make you look so good. Are we meeting after school?"

"*We'll* meet to do research." Fiona was barely opening her mouth. "You don't have to be there."

"You know she'll come," Darbie whispered to Sophie when the bell rang. "The whole bloomin' football team couldn't keep her away."

Darbie was right. After school that day, when the Flakes and Charms were all in the library finding books and websites for Fiona, Phoebe flitted from one to the other, reading over their shoulders and talking nonstop.

"The Cubans that escaped from Cuba and went to Miami in the 1960s didn't even get discriminated against like the blacks did," she said. "People thought they were heroes because they left that loser Castro to come here." She tossed her bangs. "They just set up their Little Havana and lived it up."

50

"That's not what it says," Fiona said without looking at her.

Phoebe moved to stand behind Vincent at the next computer. "Yes, it does. Right there, it basically says the Cubans that left Communist Cuba were rich and all the Americans accepted them because they kept to themselves." She looked at Maggie. "Are you rich?"

"No," Maggie said.

"Didn't think so." Phoebe stuck her tongue thoughtfully into her tooth-gap. "So how come you're not?"

Willoughby nudged Sophie. "Do we have to let her be rude?" she whispered.

Sophie almost squirmed right out of her chair. *Jesus,* she squeezed out, *help Phoebe know when to shut up.* This was definitely the hardest thing Dr. Peter had ever asked them to do.

Jimmy looked up from the book he was poring over across the table from Sophie.

"Hey, Maggie, when did you come to the United States?" he said.

"I was born here." Maggie's words thudded harder than usual. "My mom came in 1980. She was twelve."

"Our same age!" Sophie said. A character for Maggie began to form in her head. A character Liberty Lawhead could protect...

The little senora—or was it senorita?—blinked her dark, Cuban eyes up at Liberty. They begged silently for acceptance. "I know you aren't rich," Liberty said, "but you will find no discrimination here."

Sophie propped her chin in her hand. That was the problem, though. They could show that the Civil Rights Movement had worked for the Cubans, but that wouldn't make a very hot movie.

"Did you say 1980?" Nathan was at the computer farthest away from the table. His ears went radish-colored immediately as everyone looked at him.

"That's what she said." Phoebe bounced in sideways steps to get behind him. The tops of his ears got even redder as she got closer. "Did you find something good?"

"No," he said.

Sophie saw his fingers swarm over the keys like bees. But Phoebe grabbed one of his hands and stared, mouth hanging open, at the computer screen.

" 'Marielitos,' " Phoebe read. " 'Fidel Castro, Cuban dictator, allowed 125,000 people to leave the port of Mariel, Cuba, for Miami between April and October 1980. Most were unskilled and uneducated. Many were prisoners and patients from mental institutions.' " She looked like she wanted to lick her chops. "Now *that's* what I'm talkin' about."

"Maggie's mom probably wasn't like that," Jimmy said quickly.

"Hello!" Sophie said. "She was twelve years old!"

Vincent, who had been clacking away at his keyboard ever since Phoebe uttered the word *Marielitos*, said, "Dude, this *could* be good movie stuff. It says here the people in Miami didn't accept them like they did the Cubans that came in the 1960s. Even the Cubans that were already there didn't want them. They were lowlifes."

Phoebe curled one of her smiles at Maggie. "Oh," she said.

"Excuse me," Darbie said, "but Senora LaQuita is not a 'lowlife.' "

"And since we're doing a movie about her and Maggie," Fiona put in, "this Marielito thing won't work anyway."

Maggie stared at the stack of books she had just put on the table. The nothingness on her face made the back of Sophie's neck feel like it was being stuck with tacks.

"So keep looking, you guys," Sophie said.

Phoebe grabbed her hoodie, the one that said BRAT on the back. "I give you brain children one more day to find something juicy for our movie," she said. "But personally, I think this is it. See ya."

"I'm telling you, Sophie," Fiona said when Phoebe was gone, "I don't see how I'm going to hold up the Code much longer."

Sophie ran her hand over her hair-spikes. "Dr. Peter said to pray for her and not judge her," she said. "And whatever that other thing was."

"When is it supposed to start working?" Darbie said.

Maggie didn't say anything. Her silence was like a thud of its own.

"She's probably wrong about this being a good movie for our project anyway," Vincent said, still squinting at the computer screen. "Technically, the way the people in Miami treated the Marielitos isn't discrimination." He cocked his head like he was studying a math problem. "Who would want a bunch of crooks and crazies—"

"Vincent," Fiona said. She kept her eyes on Maggie.

"Yeah?"

"Stop talking."

Maggie backed away from the table, her own dark eyes so blank it was scary. "You got it messed up," she said.

"No," Vincent said, "it's right here on the Net."

"Would you hush?" Sophie turned to Maggie. "Your mom wasn't a Marielito, so it doesn't matter. We *aren't* doing the film on that—"

"It *does* matter," Maggie said. Sophie had never heard Maggie's words fall so hard. "The Internet doesn't even know—"

And then she turned with a squeal of her sneaker and was gone.

"That went well," Vincent said.

"Shut *up!*" they all said to him.

There was no time to go after Maggie because the late bus would be there any minute. Besides, Sophie reminded the Corn Flakes, when Maggie had hurt feelings, she usually needed time to simmer before people got in her face.

"I wasn't even gonna let that Phoebe girl see the website," Nathan said as they left the library. He put on the Redskins cap he always wore when he wasn't in class. It covered the ears that now looked like the inside of a watermelon.

"Let her?" Fiona said with a flare of her nostrils. "She practically took your hand off!"

"She's pushy, that one," Darbie said.

Sophie didn't remind them about the Code again. She was having a little trouble upholding it herself.

But I personally must follow the directions of Dr. Barton Gunther Prince Jr., Liberty Lawhead told herself as she left the Civil Rights for All building. Even if it doesn't feel like Diva Dramatica is truly worthy of our support.

Liberty drew herself up to her statuesque height and headed for her limousine. She must remember that Diva needed prayer — and whatever else the great doctor had said. Swinging her briefcase briskly at her side, she —

"Watch it, freak!"

Sophie pulled her backpack against herself just before it smacked into Eddie Wornom's knees. He stood between her and the late bus, eyes bugging out.

"Sorry." Sophie's voice squeaked. She made a mental note to sound more like Liberty Lawhead, or at least like Ms. Hess.

"You oughta be sorry," Eddie said, and he moved a step closer.

He smells like one big armpit, Sophie thought, holding her breath.

"It's 'cause of you I hadda hang out with Coach Nanini," Eddie said. "I coulda used that time to get in shape for basketball tryouts."

Sophie choked back the words. *There isn't that much time left in the world.*

"I'm gettin' my dad to come down here and get me off this stupid Campus Concentration thing."

"Campus Commission," Sophie said.

"Shut up! It's stupid, because *you* thought it up!"

"Eddie, Eddie, Eddie," said a familiar voice behind Sophie. "Why are you making a holy show of yourself in front of everybody?"

"Huh?" Eddie said to Darbie.

Fiona pulled Sophie back so Darbie could wedge herself between Sophie and Eddie.

"Everybody's starin' at you," Darbie said into his baffled face. "You want them to think you're an eejit?"

"What's an eejit?" Eddie said, then he lowered his head like a bull and practically snorted. "I don't care what it is, I ain't that."

Then with an *actual* snort, he stomped away.

"Did he say something heinous to you before we got here, Soph?" Fiona's gray eyes were like thunderclouds.

"He just blames me because he got caught being heinous," Sophie said.

Darbie shook her head. "You know what, Sophie? Even you couldn't dream up somebody who was that much of an ee—"

"Corn Flake Code," Fiona and Sophie droned together.

Eddie can blame me all he wants, Sophie thought as she boarded the bus. *But I'm gonna help make this a safe place for everybody to go to school.* That was what Liberty Lawhead would do.

And right now, that seemed to include Maggie. They *weren't* going to do a movie about the evil Marielitos, but there was still something about them even talking about it that had done more than make Maggie nervous. Sophie knew her fellow Corn Flake. When Maggie shut down, she was feeling extra bad inside.

That night, Sophie talked to Jesus about that. And about keeping her from smacking Zeke because he'd drawn Spider-Man webs all over her math homework while she was downstairs doing her English on the computer. And about the possibility of Eddie Wornom being miraculously turned into a Lucky Charm by Coach Virile.

She talked to Jesus about everything she could think of so she wouldn't have to talk to him about Phoebe. But finally, with Jesus' kind eyes waiting patiently, she prayed to him, *I know you love her just like you do us because she's a lost sheep and all that. I just hope you find her soon—because she's trying to take over everything like she's the boss of the world.*

She tried to leave it at that, but his eyes were still waiting.

Okay, she thought to him, *then please help me remember what that other thing was that Dr. Peter said we're supposed to do. Because it's getting way hard not to judge her.*

Sophie fell asleep praying that Jesus would make her more like Liberty Lawhead. That, she decided, was the only way this was going to work.

The Corn Flakes didn't see Maggie before school the next day, and she was late for PE, so they couldn't talk to her in the locker room, either. Willoughby said she'd been called to the office at the end of second period and left without a word. Evidently Maggie was still simmering, and Sophie was beyond squirmy. It didn't help that Phoebe pestered the Corn Flakes all during PE.

"So, did you come up with anything really delicious for our movie? It has to be something totally dramatic, you know, like someone gets thrown in jail or somebody gets murdered. We should have taken the Puerto Ricans in New York for this project. They get knifed all the time, and I know how to fake a stabbing and make phony blood that looks totally real — "

"I'll go mental if I have to listen to that girl for one more minute," Darbie said on the way to fourth period.

"We have to remember that she's lost," Sophie said without much enthusiasm.

"Not lost enough, if you ask me," Fiona said.

Sophie could hardly concentrate in math class, and when Miss Imes announced that Film Club was having an urgent meeting during lunch, Sophie gave up completely.

I bet Maggie told her we were accusing her mom of being a criminal or something, Sophie thought. *Maggie wouldn't even listen to us . . .*

Liberty Lawhead shook her head. It was so difficult to fight for a person's civil rights when that person went off angry and didn't get all the necessary information. "Ignorance is the root of prejudice," Liberty Lawhead always said. Well, she wasn't the first one to say it, but she lived by it as no other civil rights leader did in these evil times. She would simply have to find a way to make the young senorita listen to her. First she would have to find out where she was hiding —

"Soph, look who's here."

Sophie shook herself back to Fiona, who stood next to her desk, nudging her with a pencil.

"Did you find Maggie?" Sophie said.

"What? No — *look.*"

Sophie turned her gaze toward the door. Miss Imes stood in the doorway. With her was Maggie's mother.

"That can't be good," Sophie said.

"You know it," Fiona said.

Seven

When the lunch bell rang, the rest of the Film Club arrived in curious bunches and sat in the front-row seats. Sophie didn't take her eyes off Maggie's mom.

Sitting in a chair at the front of the room, Senora LaQuita wasn't wearing her usual smooth expression. Her coffee-with-milk-colored forehead was in folds, her lips pressed together in a line. Sophie had seen her angry look before, and this wasn't it.

She doesn't look like she wants to hug all of us, either, Sophie thought as she slid into a desk. She probably hadn't brought them any flan.

Sophie looked at Maggie, who sat a little apart from the rest of the group, eyes on her mom, face still showing nothing. Sophie felt squirmier than ever.

Liberty Lawhead folded her hands neatly on the desk and collected her thoughts. It was obvious that the Cuban senora was here to accuse them, the most conscientious civil rights workers on the planet, of discriminating against her and her daughter. I will simply tell her that we do not believe the information we have collected is about her, Liberty decided. Surely with her low, cool voice she would be able to soothe the senora into listening.

"Why is the cleaning lady here?" Phoebe muttered, landing in the desk next to Sophie.

Sophie glared at Phoebe. "That's Maggie's mom," she whispered.

"Oh." Phoebe leaned close to Sophie's ear. "I see a Mexican woman around here, I figure she must be on the janitor's staff."

"She's *Cuban*." Sophie's whisper-voice squeaked out of hearing range.

Miss Imes leaned against the front of her desk, and all whispers shushed. "We understand that you've uncovered some information in your research," she said, "but that there are some holes in your facts."

"I must be outta the loop," Phoebe said. "I don't know what you're talking about."

"You're about to find out," Mr. Stires said without his usual chuckle.

"Maggie?" Miss Imes said. "Why don't you start?"

This time, Sophie squirmed for Maggie. She knew that talking in front of people was *not* one of Maggie's favorite activities.

Maggie's face still didn't change as she turned her eyes on the club members and dropped her words like clumps of wet cement.

"My mom was a Marielito," she said. "But they weren't all criminals and crazy people like everybody thought."

Fiona opened her mouth, but Miss Imes said, "Just listen. Senora LaQuita has agreed to tell you what it was like for her when she left Cuba. Then there can be no mistake."

The way Senora LaQuita was pulling herself up to her full height reminded Sophie of Liberty Lawhead. It riveted Sophie's attention.

"*Gracias.* Thank you." The senora lifted her chin. "My English is no very good, but I will try to explain."

Even though Senora LaQuita pronounced "ex" like "es," Sophie wanted to cry out, *Your English is beautiful.* Beside her, Phoebe grunted.

"My father," the senora began, "he did no like Fidel Castro. Our life in Cuba—"

She pronounced it "Cooba," Sophie noticed. "It was very hard. We could no go to the church. I could no get good education because—" She frowned and said something in Spanish. "We were no like Castro. When he say anybody can go to America, my father, he build a boat for us."

Sophie suddenly felt as if she'd never really seen Senora LaQuita before. This senora was a hero, the kind movies were made about. As she told her story, the scenes unfolded in Sophie's mind.

A scene where a twelve-year-old girl and her mother and carpenter father boarded a leaky, lopsided raft held together by tires. Her face was all shiny with hope for a life in America where she could go to any church she wanted.

A scene where the boat sank with Miami in sight—and where the girl woke up in a hospital, surrounded by people who babbled in a language she couldn't understand.

A scene where she and her mother sat in a city of tents and mourned her father, drowned just a few feet from the Florida shore.

A scene where her mother tried to find work, but even Cuban Americans didn't trust her because she had arrived with the Marielitos. They were angry with *her* because other people from her country had been in Castro's prisons.

And a scene where the frightened twelve-year-old Cuban girl learned her first English word. "Scum," said the American officer as he jerked his thumb toward her and her mother. She only had to see the man's face to know what it meant.

The room was silent when Senora LaQuita finished talking. Sophie could hear her own heartbeat pounding in her ears.

"I think you've found your story of discrimination," Miss Imes said to the group. "Thank you — *gracias*, Senora LaQuita, for sharing your story with us."

Before anyone else could speak, Phoebe said, "Yeah, thanks. That story'll make a great movie. When do we start?"

Did somebody die and leave you in charge? Sophie thought. The back of her neck was alive with prickles.

The Film Club agreed to meet the next day, Saturday, at Darbie's. But the Corn Flakes spent Friday night there to paint each other's toenails and write letters to Kitty and make sure their Maggie didn't think they were heinous.

"I wasn't mad at you," Maggie said while Willoughby applied an exact replica of Sponge Bob to each of Maggie's two big toenails. "I just couldn't explain it like my mom did."

"She was so beautiful," Sophie said.

"Your mom has great nails," Willoughby said.

Darbie snickered. "I don't think that's what Sophie meant, Willoughby."

Willoughby blinked her almost-Frisbee-size eyes, and the Corn Flakes sent up a chorus of giggling snorts. Then they linked pinkies just because.

The next day, Sophie was glad they'd done that, because working on the movie definitely didn't feel like Corn Flakes Productions. Not with so many other people involved.

Actually — not with Phoebe involved.

Phoebe wanted to do every scene six times until it was perfect, even though they were just playing with them to get ideas written down.

She said things like, "I want to try it again, only with Cuban Girl here."

"Her name is Maggie," the Corn Flakes told her nine times. By the tenth time, they all shouted it together, with the boys joining in—even Nathan.

A smelling-something-funny smile spread across Phoebe's face.

"That was good. You guys should all be off-camera yelling during the scene where I get in Cuban Girl's—Maggie's—face in the Food Stamp Office."

"Yelling what?" Darbie said.

"You know, stuff like 'Get a job or go back where you came from, moocher.'" Phoebe looked at Willoughby. "You're a Rah-Rah Girl. You know how to yell."

Willoughby gave a nervous half-yip. "I don't think I can yell *that*."

"It's acting," Phoebe said. "Okay, I'll do the scene, and when I wave my hand, you just yell stuff like you agree with me."

"You know," Fiona's pink bow of a mouth twisted into a knot even as she spoke, "Sophie is usually the director."

Sophie folded her arms. "Yeah, if you don't mind—"

"Just let me show you," Phoebe said. "You—" She looked at Maggie. "Sit in this chair. I'm behind the desk, and you just came in asking for food stamps."

She half pushed Maggie into a dining room chair. Maggie looked down at the table. Once again, all expression disappeared.

"We'll work on your part later. Let's just do mine." Phoebe leaned back in the chair and narrowed her eyes until Sophie was sure they would cross. "I am so sick of you people," she said.

Willoughby yipped. Darbie put a hand on her arm. "She's acting," she said.

"Miami isn't even an American city anymore," the Phoebe character said. "Once you people started running out the whites, that was the end of anything American." She crawled her forearms halfway across the table. "I bet somebody's payin' you under the table so you don't have to pay taxes, and here you are trying to get money from *our* taxpayers. The *real* Americans."

Phoebe waved her hand, but nobody said anything. Sophie didn't even know what she was talking about. Besides, she was frozen by the hatred Phoebe was acting out.

"Nobody wants to live near you people," the Phoebe character said, her voice rising. "All the whites are running from you aliens. That's what you are, you know, trying to make us all speak Spanish and running for office so you can turn Miami into another Cuba. No!"

Phoebe banged her fist on the table and made Darbie's aunt Emily's crystal vase jitter in place.

"*Some* people might help you, but I intend to remain civilized! Otherwise, they're gonna let anybody in here. Any scum, do you hear me?"

"*What in the world?*"

Sophie jittered like the crystal vase. Aunt Emily crossed the dining room with one manicured hand over her mouth. She was what Mama called a true Southern lady, and right now she looked like she was about to faint like one.

"Why am I hearing this kind of talk?" she said in her very-proper Virginia accent.

"Phoebe was just acting a part for our flick, Aunt Em," Darbie said.

"Cool," Phoebe said. "I had you convinced." She turned to Darbie. "Did you get any of that on film?"

"I'm not so sure I like this movie," Aunt Emily said.

"You're not actually supposed to like it." Vincent's voice cracked. "It's supposed to educate you and make you think."

"Or make you mad," Fiona said.

Aunt Emily tapped a finger against her lips. "I think it will."

As hard as it was, Sophie had to agree with her. Phoebe was an amazing actor. She might *know* it like no other, but she was good.

Even Fiona nodded her approval as Aunt Emily left the room.

"You should be in real movies," Willoughby said.

"I will be someday," Phoebe said. "Wait 'til you see what I do in the tent-city scene." She looked at Fiona. "That's at your house tomorrow?"

"We have to switch to plan B," Fiona said. "My dad said he doesn't want us putting up a bunch of tents in the yard and messing up the lawn."

"No problem," Phoebe said. "We'll do it at my house. My dad could care less about the lawn." She curled her lip into that smile. "You guys really think I'm good?"

"Hello!" Willoughby said. "Look—I chewed off two fingernails!"

There was smiling. Something, Sophie thought, had kind of changed. Still, she felt squirmy.

After Sunday school the next day, the Corn Flakes talked nonstop about Phoebe.

"We have to admit she's an incredible actress," Fiona said. "Even though I hate to because she thinks she's better than the rest of us."

Willoughby tilted her head. "I think she started being nicer after we gave her all those compliments."

"She did?" Darbie said.

"She invited us to her house," Sophie said. "That might be Phoebe being nice."

"What's 'nice' for Phoebe is, like, almost heinous for one of us." Fiona put up her hand. "That's not against the Code. I'm just agreeing."

Sophie felt the shiver of an idea, something Liberty Lawhead herself might come up with. "You know what?" she said. "I just remembered that other thing Dr. Peter said. We're supposed to appreciate her for her good stuff."

"Like tell her she's all that as an actress?" Willoughby said.

"Yeah," Sophie said. "'Cause like you just said, she was a little nicer when we did that."

Fiona pulled back and frowned. "Dr. Peter said we shouldn't try to change her."

"Maybe that's not changing her," Darbie said. "I acted like an eejit when I first met all of you — worse than Phoebe — but I wasn't really like that inside. I just did it because I was all angry and afraid." Sophie thought Darbie's eyes got a little misty. "But then you accepted me, and now I'm—"

"Fabulous!" Willoughby said. She gave her happy-poodle yip.

Sophie didn't get to find out if anybody else agreed. Daddy appeared and sent her to the primary room to sit with Zeke because he was having a meltdown. His third one that day.

Sophie had to feed him an entire roll of Smarties she'd been saving, even her favorite green ones, just to get him calmed down from the fit he was having because somebody else was playing with the Noah's ark set. She tried not to think about what Tuesday afternoon was going to be like.

It was easy to forget about that the minute Fiona's grandfather, Boppa, pulled up to Phoebe's house that afternoon in the SUV loaded with the Corn Flakes and their tents.

"I see why Phoebe's father doesn't care about his lawn," Fiona said. "He doesn't have one."

Sophie couldn't actually tell if there was any grass around the house with the peely green paint. There was something on every square inch of the ground—old lawn mowers and gas cans and something that might have been a car once.

"Where are we going to put up tents?" Darbie said.

"Someplace safe, I hope." Boppa's caterpillar eyebrows almost met in the middle. "I think I'll stick around and watch the rehearsal."

"That would be fabulous, Boppa," Sophie said. Something about Phoebe's yard was making her want to stay in the car.

Phoebe bolted out the front door wearing a faded poncho that looked like somebody had worn it the last time ponchos were in style. Nathan, Vincent, and Jimmy trailed out after her. Nathan's face was so red, Sophie couldn't tell where it stopped and his Redskins cap started.

"I thought you'd never get here," Phoebe said. "The call was for two o'clock and it's five after."

"The call?" Fiona said, lips already bunching up.

"That's theater talk," Phoebe said. "I can give you a lesson on that later."

"I thought you said she was getting nicer," Darbie whispered to Sophie as they followed Phoebe to the backyard.

Fiona grunted. Maggie didn't say anything. She hadn't said anything since they'd pulled in.

"We have to keep giving her compliments," Sophie whispered back.

"Great space for the tent scene," Vincent said.

There wasn't as much stuff in the backyard. Just one rusty wheelbarrow and a chicken coop minus the chickens.

"They all died," Phoebe told them.

It took a few minutes for the girls to get their tents up near where the boys had already pitched theirs. Boppa stood on the back porch until the door creaked open. A man almost as stick-skinny as Vincent came out.

"Ned Bunting." Boppa stuck out his hand.

"Buck Karnes." The man shook Boppa's hand absently as he squinted at the kids. Sophie was amazed how much Phoebe looked like him. The only thing missing was a gap between his two front teeth.

"Don't be touchin' none of my stuff, Phoebe," he said.

Okay, so the gap wasn't missing. But there was something—in his eyes—that Phoebe didn't have in hers.

"We aren't gonna touch any of your precious stuff," Phoebe said without looking at him.

"I'd be afraid to," Fiona murmured to Sophie.

Sophie knelt to check her tent spikes. Jimmy was suddenly there beside her. "Phoebe must be really poor," he whispered. "I kinda feel sorry for her." His blue eyes looked sad.

Sophie decided she liked that about him. "We're all trying to tell her she's fabulous and all that," she whispered back. "She seems nicer when we do that."

Jimmy nodded his blond head toward the back porch. "I don't think that'll work on her dad. He's pretty mean. You shoulda heard him yelling at her before you came."

Even now, Mr. Karnes' voice was way louder than it needed to be for Boppa, who was standing right next to him.

"This is some thing they picked to do a movie about," he said. "Cubans. I told Phoebe all they're good at is highjackin' planes."

He grinned like he'd just delivered a hilarious punch line. His lip even curled back like Phoebe's. Boppa didn't smile with him.

"I remember back in '80 when Castro let all his rejects go," Mr. Karnes went on. "It was all over the news, them washin' up right on those fancy beaches in Miami and spongin' off

Americans the minute they got here." He spat off the side of the porch. "I heard any white person wants to stay livin' down there has to have bars on their windows."

"I don't think so," Boppa said.

"Oh, yeah. Crime's worse down there than in New York City. Cubans are dealing drugs and counterfeiting money and robbing tourists."

"Excuse me," Fiona said.

Sophie sucked in her breath. Fiona was marching toward the porch.

Eight

In case you haven't noticed," Fiona said before she even reached Phoebe's father, "our friend Maggie is Cuban. I'm sure she doesn't appreciate you saying things like that."

"Who's a Cuban?" Mr. Karnes' eyes darted across the yard like he was looking for a rattlesnake.

Darbie stepped in front of Maggie. Jimmy was right beside her. Sophie was stuck between wanting to cover Maggie's ears and wishing she could escape into Liberty Lawhead on the spot.

"Fiona," Boppa said, "let me handle this."

"You better do it quick," Fiona said. "Before I —"

"Fiona," Boppa said.

Their beloved Boppa didn't raise his voice that often. When he did, everybody shifted into obedience mode. Fiona backed down from the porch.

"You kids get to work," Boppa said. He looked at Mr. Karnes. "Could we talk privately? Inside?"

Mr. Karnes shrugged, and they disappeared inside the house. Nobody said anything for a minute. Even Phoebe was quiet as she stared at the door.

"I wondered where you got that big speech yesterday," Vincent finally said to Phoebe. "Now I know."

"You sounded just like your father," Darbie said.

Fiona snorted. "Go figure."

Phoebe took a bow. "Thank you," she said. "I get my material wherever I can."

"Do you believe him?"

Sophie jumped. It was the first thing Maggie had said since they'd arrived. And Maggie's face wasn't blank anymore. Her eyes were hard and shiny, like wet stones.

Phoebe looked as startled as Sophie felt, but only for a few seconds. Then something hard came into her eyes too. That final piece made her look identical to her father.

"My dad's a jerk," she said. "I never even listen to him except when I need an example for a character. When I told him what we were doing our movie on, he just came out with this whole monologue—"

"Then you don't believe him," Sophie said quickly. She could practically feel Maggie growing stiffer by the second.

"Who cares?" Phoebe said. "It's all about the part for me."

"*We* care if Maggie gets her feelings hurt." Fiona's nostrils were flared so wide, Sophie was sure she herself could have crawled in. "Your father needs to apologize to her."

"Right," Phoebe said. "Like I can make him."

"You probably can't," Vincent said. He sounded like he was talking about a math problem. "On the meanness scale, he's about a—"

"So, do you guys want to do this scene or what?" Jimmy said.

Sophie decided she liked him for that too. But as they set up the "scum word" scene, Sophie couldn't help wondering—

Was Phoebe really that good an actor? Had she really just played her father yesterday when she yelled at Maggie?

Or did she believe what she was saying?

She can't even remember Maggie's name half the time, Sophie thought. *And she just automatically assumed Senora LaQuita was the cleaning lady.*

71

Not only that, but Phoebe pushed Maggie around like she was her servant or something. Even now, she was saying, "You—get behind Fiona since she's your mom and act like you're scared. Do something besides just stare."

"You know what, Phoebe?" Fiona said. "Why don't you just worry about your own acting and let Maggie do her thing?"

"Works for me," Vincent said.

"I'm just trying to make this thing sensational," Phoebe said. "You guys could learn so much from me."

Liberty Lawhead drew in a deep breath. This was the hardest case she had ever come up against. It was so much easier when the bad guys were totally bad and there was no mistaking their heinous-ness. But when someone was sometimes right, but was so hard to listen to, and when that same someone didn't come right out and say she, well, hated Cubans, what was she to do?

"I must remember what Dr. Barton Gunther Prince Jr. told us," Liberty said out loud so she would be sure to hear herself. *"We must pray and not judge. God will make it clear to us when we need to speak out."*

"How does that fit into this scene?" Phoebe said.

I think it fits into every scene, Sophie thought.

She looked at Maggie and wished the hardness would disappear from her friend's eyes.

But that look stayed with Maggie over the next several days.

They practiced at Sophie's after school Tuesday because of Zeke. When Sophie set him up on the back patio with his Spider-Man toys, he swept them all off the table with one arm and wailed that he wanted to be in the movie.

Phoebe said Maggie should watch him because wasn't that what "you people are good at?" It didn't sound like a compliment to Sophie, and it obviously didn't to Maggie, either. She looked so hard at Phoebe, Jimmy jumped in to sling Zeke over his shoulder and carried him around through the whole rehearsal. Sophie *really* liked that about him.

But Zeke was so wired after everybody left, he grabbed the plates off the dinner table and flung two of them like Frisbees before Sophie could stop him.

"I'm staging a protest!" he said.

No more rehearsals at their house, Mama said.

Wednesday, Phoebe complained because the rest of the girls went to Bible study instead of meeting to practice.

"So come with us," Sophie said.

Three different Corn Flakes poked her in the back.

"Me go to church?" Phoebe said. "Nah. Religion is a bunch of hooey." She looked at Maggie. "Do you go to this Bible study thing too?"

"Yes," Maggie said woodenly.

"Why wouldn't she?" Fiona said.

Fiona's voice got colder every time she spoke to Phoebe. Pretty soon, she was going to frost Phoebe's eyebrows.

"I thought the Cubans did, like, weird rituals and stuff. I read it in some of that stuff Vincent printed out."

Sophie made a mental note to tell Vincent to stop with the Internet, already.

"I'm a Christian," Maggie said, staring at Phoebe.

Phoebe shrugged. "Okay. Don't have a seizure."

During Bible study that day, Dr. Peter had a fall feast for them, with grapes and bread and apples and pumpkin squares. There was a lot of giggling and grape peeling, but they didn't have time to discuss their problems like they usually did.

That was okay with Sophie. She wanted to talk to Dr. Peter alone about it, and she hung back after everybody else left. She especially didn't want Maggie to hear—just in case Maggie wasn't catching all the little remarks Phoebe muttered under her breath. It would be okay after she told Dr. Peter everything, she just knew it.

"We really, really tried to appreciate her and not judge her and stuff," Sophie told Dr. Peter after she'd brought him up to speed, "and I've been sort of praying for her. She's nicer to the rest of us now, but not to Maggie." She wrinkled her nose to push her glasses up, the way Dr. Peter always did. "Maybe she's just naturally mean that way, you know, like her father."

Dr. Peter wrinkled his nose too. "I don't think any kid is just naturally mean," he said. "Usually a girl acts mean because she's angry or scared."

"But we don't have to keep trying if what we're doing isn't working, do we?" Sophie could hear her voice squeaking up hopefully. "It isn't fair to Maggie."

"Just because it doesn't look like it's working doesn't mean it isn't," Dr. Peter said. "I'm not saying you have to make Phoebe a member of the Corn Flakes, but you've made a commitment to work with her on this project."

Sophie squirmed.

"And I'm not saying you should let her get away with being mean to Maggie. I'm concerned about that part. If Maggie is having trouble with it, you need to bring in some grown-ups. That isn't busting people, you know."

"Maggie keeps saying she's fine." Sophie ran her hand over her fuzzy do. "But she doesn't really know how bad it is. And I don't want her to find out."

Dr. Peter leaned back in his beanbag and put his hands behind his head. "Basically, Sophie-Lophie-Loodle, you want me to give you permission to cut this girl loose."

Sophie didn't say anything. The back of her neck prickled. This wasn't going at *all* the way she wanted it to.

"That's your decision," Dr. Peter said. "You can try to protect Maggie from experiencing prejudice, and that's a very nice thing to want to do. Or—" He rubbed his hands together. "You can do what Jesus did and help Maggie stand up for herself and help Phoebe understand that what she's doing is—what's that word you like?"

"Heinous," Sophie said.

"And you can do it the way the Corn Flakes always do—with honesty and respect—all that good Code stuff."

The prickling on Sophie's neck was going out of control. "I told you it isn't working," she said.

Dr. Peter squinted a little behind his glasses. "Keep doing what you're doing, Loodle. And do two more things."

"I don't want to do two more things, Dr. Peter!" Sophie said. "I just want you to tell me it's okay to dump her!"

"I can always count on you to be honest, can't I?" He shook his head. "But I have to be honest too. That isn't the right thing to do. It would make you a Pharisee."

"Me?" Sophie said.

"Maggie isn't a lost sheep. She has a Shepherd to show her who she is. But your Phoebe is one. Most people who need that much attention are acting out their lostness. And most people who exhibit prejudice are afraid." He leaned toward Sophie. "I wouldn't say this to most kids your age, but you're special this way, Soph. You get it. Think of Phoebe as a lost lamb instead of a bossy girl who doesn't like Cuban people. Isn't that what Jesus was trying to tell the Pharisees in that story?"

"But I'm not like them!" Sophie said.

"No, you're not," Dr. Peter said. "But sometimes a little Pharisee-itis can sneak in."

The back of Sophie's neck felt like it had a cactus stuck to it.

"I have to go." For the first time ever, Sophie was glad to leave Dr. Peter. She'd never imagined it could happen, but Dr. Peter just didn't understand.

And he wasn't the only one. That night while Lacie did double duty with Zeke and told Sophie she owed her big-time, Mama came into Sophie's room for a talk. Sophie saw a tiny line between Mama's eyebrows, and she knew whatever her mom had to say wouldn't make her any happier.

Still, Sophie shared the only package of Smarties she'd kept out of Zeke's clutches and even gave Mama the green ones, just in case it might sweeten things up some.

But Mama delivered bad news anyway: there were to be no more rehearsals for the Cuban movie project at *any* of the Corn Flakes' houses.

"I know the movie is important," Mama said before Sophie could protest, "but it has some pretty rough scenes. None of us Corn Flake parents feel like we can supervise so many of you. You know, the boys. And your new friend."

"But we could still rehearse at Phoebe's," Sophie said. "Her dad didn't care—"

She trailed off as Mama stopped with the last green Smartie almost to her mouth. "Absolutely not," she said. "Boppa was very concerned about that situation. You girls are wonderful about bringing out the best in people, but we think that should be done where you have better adult supervision."

The way Mama said it made Sophie wonder if all the parents had memorized the same speech and were right now delivering it to their own Corn Flakes. At least Daddy wasn't here, putting in a bunch of sports stuff she never understood.

Suddenly, Sophie felt like she was being pulled in two directions like a Gumby doll.

In one direction was the hope that her parents would say she couldn't be around Phoebe ever again. Then she wouldn't have to do all the stuff Dr. Peter told her to do.

But in the other direction was their project. *This is all Phoebe's fault!* she thought.

"How are we going to practice then?" Sophie said. Her voice entered a whole new squeak-zone.

"We talked to the school. You have permission to practice on the school grounds after classes. They'll have an adult there." Mama smiled her wispy smile. "You can even take your camera if you keep it in Mr. Stires' room when you aren't using it."

Sophie wondered if Mama had checked with Daddy about that one. Taking the camera to school was *huge*. But even that didn't help. Sophie choked the Smarties package closed with a twist. This was getting less and less like a Corn Flakes Production every single second.

"Dream Girl," Mama patted the pillow next to her, "join me for a minute."

Sophie flopped back against the cushions.

"Are you feeling a little bit like everything's upside down right now?" Mama said.

I'm feeling a lot that way, Sophie opened her mouth to say.

But then she stopped. Daddy said they were supposed to keep Mama from getting upset, not give her more stuff to worry about.

So instead, she said, "Want some more Smarties?"

There was a scream from the direction of the bathroom.

"Mo-om!" Lacie yelled. "I can't be responsible for what I'm going to do to that kid when you get me out of here!"

Sophie could hear Zeke taking the steps down two at a time.

"You want Lacie or Zeke?" Mama said.

Sophie took Lacie. Once she'd climbed up on a chair to get the bathroom door key off the ledge and released a frothing Lacie from Spider-Man's prison, she retreated to her room again.

Liberty Lawhead curled up in the corner of her jail cell. I must remain strong, she told herself. Even though the powerful people who don't understand keep squeezing me in, tighter and tighter. I must continue to reveal the truth about such things as Diva Dramatica's prejudice—

"And about Dr. Peter being wrong," Sophie said into the pillow over her head. "And all the parents being wrong."

She tried to imagine Jesus, but all she could see was a strange progression of people who might supervise their next rehearsal. Miss Imes. Coach Yates. Mr. Janitor Man.

"This is just heinous," Fiona said after school Friday as the Corn Flakes trailed with the camera out toward the field hockey practice area.

It was a bright, crisp November day, perfect for filming, but Sophie nodded at Fiona. This situation gave heinous a whole new meaning.

"I just hope there aren't a lot of kids out there watching us," Darbie said.

Willoughby nodded grimly. "It would be just like the Corn Pops to spy on us and steal our ideas."

As they stepped onto the edge of the field, the Lucky Charms joined them.

"That's the least of our worries," Vincent said.

He pointed toward a small set of bleachers, and Sophie groaned out loud. There was Eddie Wornom, doing something to a bleacher seat with a screwdriver big enough to be seen across the field.

"What's he doing here?" Jimmy said. Sophie thought he suddenly looked all protective. "I thought he had Campus Commission."

Sophie said, "He does, only where's Coach Nanini?"

"I'm not a coach today," said a high-for-a-guy voice behind them. "I'm a Hollywood producer."

Sophie turned to see him wiggling his one big eyebrow and peering at them over the tops of his sunglasses.

"Who's in charge of this production?" he said. "You, Little Bit?"

Sophie grinned. She wished Phoebe'd heard that. This was the first decent thing that had happened all day. "Are you babysitting us?" said another voice.

Phoebe trotted up, her own pink-glittered plastic sunglasses riding on top of her head.

"I'm supervising," Coach Nanini said.

Phoebe shook her bangs out of her eyes. "We don't really need supervising," she said. "What we need are some extras."

"Extra what?" Fiona said.

Her voice could have freeze-dried Phoebe's lips. Sophie rubbed the back of her neck.

"Extra people," Phoebe said. "I need to teach you some vocabulary. Anyway, I just don't see how we can stage a riot scene with just us." She tossed her head dramatically. "These working conditions!"

"I can create the illusion with the camera," Vincent said. "So it'll look like we have, like, a cast of thousands."

"We want real," Phoebe said. "Not a delusion."

"Illusion," Fiona said. "I need to teach you some vocab—"

"We should get started!" Sophie said, although she would have loved to let Fiona finish that sentence and more. Her neck was on fire with prickles.

"We still need at least one other person to play another cop." Phoebe pointed toward the bleachers. "What about Chubbo?"

"You mean Mr. Wornom?" Coach Nanini said.

All of the Corn Flakes and the Lucky Charms shook their heads, but Coach slowly nodded his.

"Mr. Wornom!" he shouted. "We need you over here."

Eddie turned, then stuck the tool he'd been using into his back pocket and lumbered toward them.

"He'll do," Phoebe said.

"We're putting Eddie in our movie?" Willoughby whispered to Sophie.

Sophie didn't answer.

Nine

❋ ⬠ ✺

ow about no!" Fiona said through clenched teeth as Eddie approached.

"So much for a totally class flick," Darbie said through hers.

Willoughby just stifled a shriek. Maggie didn't say anything. Neither did her face. Sophie chomped down on her own tongue.

Phoebe pranced at Eddie's side before he even got to them. "Have you had any acting experience?" she said.

"He only knows one way to act," Nathan muttered.

Eddie looked Phoebe up and down like she was a space alien. "I ain't no actor," he said.

"You've got the perfect look for the part, though," Phoebe said.

"Oh, yes," Darbie whispered to Sophie. "He'll fit right into a scene about a shower of savages."

Eddie opened his mouth, and Sophie covered her ears. But to her surprise, he looked at Coach Nanini and said, "Do I gotta?"

Say no! Sophie wanted to blurt out.

Coach Nanini adjusted his sunglasses and folded his ham-like arms. "You don't have to, but it would sure prove to me that you're getting this whole help-and-cooperate thing."

Eddie glared at Sophie as if she alone were responsible for this torture. "Will it get me off earlier?" he said.

"The only thing that will get me out of your life, Mr. Wornom," Coach Nanini said, "is for you to show me a genuine change in your attitude."

Now we'll see if he can act, Sophie thought.

"Come on, you'll be a natural," Phoebe said. "You get to yell at them."

She pointed to the Corn Flakes. Eddie's face lit up. "And you can spit over your shoulder," Phoebe told him. "I saw cops do that when they came to our house because people complained about our chickens."

"Just confine your spitting to the ground, Mr. Wornom," Coach Nanini said. "If a loogie hits skin, you go back ten steps."

A slow grin scrunched up Eddie's cheeks. Sophie felt her eyes bulging almost to her glasses as he said, "Okay. I'll do it. Do I get a gun?"

While Phoebe explained to him that, unfortunately, there would be no weapons involved, Coach Nanini motioned Sophie over to him.

"It's still up to you whether you let him in, Little Bit," he said. "I won't let him mess up your movie. But having him help is what the Round Table program is all about, right?"

Sophie didn't remember anybody on the council ever saying *that*. She just felt squirmy and squeezed and prickly at the same time. *But Liberty Lawhead raised up her chin. If she had to think of the lowest of the low as people with rights, who should be called "Mr." instead of "Scum," then she would. That was the price one paid in being a leader.*

"Places for the riot scene, everyone," Sophie said. "The role of the policeman will be played by Eddie Wornom."

"Good choice, Little Bit," Coach Nanini said as the group scattered to set up. "You're on the top shelf looking down."

Jimmy produced a box he'd brought for Sophie to stand on so Liberty Lawhead could be seen. Maggie/Senorita stood on the ground beside her, head still as high as Sophie's, and Nathan and Eddie parked behind them as the two police officers. The crowd gathered in front of them, with Phoebe right in the middle, already warming up to shout protests in the middle of Liberty's speech. Vincent stood apart with the camera. It was his turn to film, and he'd been dying for the chance.

Sophie took a deep breath while Phoebe gave the Corn Flakes some final pointers. All the things the grown-ups had said squeezed her again.

How am I supposed to not judge them and bring out the best in them, Sophie thought, *with Eddie Wornom standing there hating me and Maggie looking like she would rather be having a heart transplant—*

"What's the matter?" Phoebe said to her. "You got gas?"

Eddie sputtered out a loud, nasty laugh.

"Okay, action," Sophie said.

"Hey, by the way," Vincent said. "Nice camera, Sophie." Then he gave her a thumbs-up that he was shooting.

"It is dangerous to deny rights to individuals," Sophie/ Liberty cried out to the crowd in her best Ms. Hess voice, "by lumping them into a group and judging each by the guilt of a few. Only one percent of the Marielitos are actual criminals, and this girl and her mother are certainly not among them."

She put her hand on Maggie/Senorita's shoulder. The words were still pulsing through her as if they had been real.

"They're all guilty!" Phoebe shouted from the crowd. "They all carry guns! Frisk her—they're probably using her to smuggle in weapons!"

Phoebe charged toward Maggie, dragging a reluctant Willoughby with her. Right on cue, Nathan stepped forward and said, "That's far enough. Get back."

"Everybody start rioting," Phoebe said under her breath to Jimmy and the Flakes.

They rushed toward Liberty/Sophie and Maggie/Senorita just like they were supposed to, with the two "cops" pushing them back with their hands. Officer Eddie, Sophie noticed, seemed to be enjoying grabbing Phoebe by the arm and flinging her skinny body from side to side. Just as Sophie/Liberty put her arms around a very stiff Maggie/Senorita to protect her, Phoebe's voice swelled above it all.

"Keep your hands off me, pig!" her character screamed into Officer Eddie's face. "I know my rights!"

Eddie's eyes squinted until they were mere poke holes in his face.

"Who you callin' a pig?" he said.

"You!" Phoebe's character shouted. "We're the ones you should protect, not them, you fat excuse for law enforcement!"

"Shut up!" Eddie shouted back.

In the instant that he reached for his back pocket, Sophie knew Eddie wasn't acting, and that he didn't know Phoebe was.

"Go ahead, hit me!" Phoebe's character cried. "I'll sue you for police brutality."

Eddie's face went purple. He yanked the giant screwdriver out of his pocket, fist clenched around the handle, and drew his arm back.

"Phoebe, look out!" Sophie screamed.

Suddenly things seemed to shift into slow motion. Phoebe threw up her arms and shouted, "Cut!" Coach Nanini ran for Eddie, but before he could get there, Eddie flung the screwdriver, and it tumbled end over end through the air, landing just inches from Maggie's foot. Eddie dived for it, landing on his belly with a grunt.

Everyone else froze. All except Phoebe, who went after Eddie, teeth bared like tiger fangs. Coach Nanini hauled Eddie out of the way and lifted him to his feet, but Phoebe kept coming at him, clawing the air with her fingernails.

"Guys," Coach Nanini said, "this is one time when you can grab a girl."

Nathan and Jimmy got hold of Phoebe from behind and pulled her back, dodging her heels as she kicked at them.

"What are you, some kind of crazy method actor?" Phoebe screamed at Eddie. "You coulda hit me!"

"I was *tryin'* to hit you!" Eddie screamed back. "You called me a pig!"

"I don't think anger management is working too well," Fiona muttered to Sophie.

Sophie shook her head. *And Mama thought we'd be safer here.*

Coach Nanini got Eddie calmed down enough to send him off to the locker room to be dealt with later, but it wasn't that easy to handle Phoebe. She carried on for a good two minutes before Nathan and Jimmy could let her go without her trying to take them out. When they did set her free at Coach Nanini's command, she shot off like a missile toward the gym building.

"She'll go right into the boys' locker room, that one," Darbie murmured.

"I'd kind of like to see that, actually," Fiona said.

Willoughby let out a yip-giggle, and then she couldn't seem to stop. Darbie snorted, and Fiona just collapsed on the ground.

"What's the deal?" Jimmy said to Coach Nanini.

"Son, don't ask me to explain women," Coach said, "because I won't even try."

As he jogged off toward the locker room, Sophie felt a relief giggle coming up in her own throat, until she looked at Maggie.

Maggie wasn't laughing, but her face finally had something in it. Something that made her eyes swim and made her hug her arms around herself. Something that made her look afraid.

"Stop, you guys," Sophie said.

The Corn Flakes cut off their laughter in mid-giggle.

Sophie held out her hand to Vincent for the camera. "We're through rehearsing for the day. See you guys tomorrow."

"You don't want to see the footage?" Vincent said as he handed it to her. "I got some great stuff—"

"Come on," Jimmy said. "I think this is some kind of girl thing."

After Jimmy herded Vincent away, with Nathan several red-eared yards ahead of them, the Flakes huddled around their Maggie. Attempts at comfort flew out of every mouth.

"She was only acting—"

"When she got really mad, it was about Eddie—"

"You almost can't blame her—he threw a big ol' screwdriver thing at her!"

"Don't be shook over her, Mags—"

"You've got us."

But Maggie stopped it all with just one sentence. "She hates me like that too."

For a long moment, nobody said it wasn't true. And when Willoughby tried, things began to fire out of Maggie—not in thuds, but in flaming cannonballs she'd obviously been storing up for a long time.

"When you aren't looking she gives me hate stares," Maggie said. "And when you can't hear her, like when she gets me off away from you and tries to tell me how to act, she says other stuff too, like why do I always smell like beans and does my mother have a gun in our house and is my father in prison." She took a breath. "And when she gets all in my face when we're practicing and everybody says she's such a good actor, that's not acting. She means it. Just like she meant it when Eddie threw that thing at her. And now I'm scared because I know how bad she can hate. And I don't even want to be in this movie, even if I have to take an F."

Maggie sucked in another big gulp of air. Sophie knew that was a lot for her to say.

"Okay, that's it," Fiona said. "We are so not putting up with this anymore. I say we go to Miss Imes right now and tell her Phoebe has to go."

"No," Maggie said.

"We have to," Sophie said. "Mags, this is so unfair." She found herself shaking, and she knew even Liberty Lawhead would do the same. This was scarier than anything.

Dr. Peter had said that when Maggie started having trouble with it, it was time for a grown-up.

But Maggie was shaking her head so hard, her hair was slapping against her cheeks.

"When you try to stop people like her, they just treat you worse," she said. "My mother said so. That's why she left Miami when I was a baby and came here." Maggie's voice trembled. "I just want to stay away from that Phoebe girl."

"But you can't take an F, Mags," Fiona said.

"Why can't we just keep Maggie away from her?" Darbie said. "All the scenes she's in with Mags are done. We can do the rest on the sly."

"That's sneaking," Maggie said. "It's against the Corn Flake Code."

"It's the only way to protect you if you won't go to Miss Imes or somebody." Fiona put her hands on Maggie's shoulders. "You have to make a choice."

"Come on, Mags." Willoughby sounded like she was about to cry. "We're the Corn Flakes."

Whatever that meant to Maggie seemed to settle over her, and she nodded slowly. "Okay," she said. "I'll finish the movie. Just keep her away from me."

Pinkies came out for a solemn promise.

Finally, Sophie thought. *We can just get away from Phoebe and not feel bad about it.*

But even as they linked fingers, Sophie felt something that wasn't a squirm or a prickle or a squeeze. It was just a deep feeling that something was wrong somehow.

That feeling faded a little as they sat on the bleachers and made a plan for keeping Maggie safe from Phoebe. The only thing Maggie insisted on was that Sophie be with her all the time.

Darbie gave a soft snort. "Do you really think Sophie is the person to have with you if Phoebe starts scratching your face with her fingernails like she tried with Eddie?"

"I can keep her from hurting me outside by myself," Maggie said. "But Sophie can keep her from hurting me inside." She turned her frightened eyes on Sophie. "Stay with me all the time."

Sophie nodded until she could get some words out. "I won't leave your side at school when we're not in class, Mags," she said.

As Liberty Lawhead followed her Civil Rights for All team toward their building, with the terrified senorita at her side, she tried to raise her chin and straighten her shoulders and draw up to her statuesque height.

But there was a deep feeling. Something she had never felt tugging at her insides before. If she hadn't known herself so well, she would have thought it was doubt.

Willoughby gave Sophie a tiny push toward the open bus door.

"Where's Maggie?" Sophie said.

"Boppa's giving her a ride home," Darbie said. "She'll be safe."

Liberty Lawhead sighed as she stepped into the backseat of her limo. She must get her confidence back. They had made a decision, and they must follow through—

But as Sophie turned her face to the bus window, she saw herself reflected there, not Liberty Lawhead. Her own brown eyes were as frightened as Maggie's.

She closed them and tried to get Liberty back. But there were only the kind eyes there.

"I think we better talk when I get home," she whispered to Jesus. "Or there's gonna be big trouble."

Ten

Sophie decided to go straight to her room when she got home and imagine Jesus. She was way too confused to do anything else.

But when she walked into the kitchen, Daddy was home, and he had that face on that Lacie always said was like the coach's at halftime when the team was losing bad.

And Zeke was the player he was blaming.

Zeke sat on the snack bar, legs swinging and eyes lowered. Daddy leaned over him so that their faces almost touched. Lacie stood just inside the open pantry closet like she was looking for the perfect snack to go with watching their little brother get busted. But Sophie had a feeling she was just trying to stay out of sight.

Sophie joined her.

"Now, buddy," Daddy said. "Mama tells me you didn't behave like a big guy while I was gone."

"Ya think?" Lacie whispered to Sophie.

"You want to tell me what you did?" Daddy said.

"I did some stuff," Zeke said. Sophie could tell he was hardly opening his mouth. "I don't remember all of it, though."

"Did you write all over Sophie's math paper?"

"No. Spider-Man drew webs on it."

"Did you lock Lacie in the bathroom?"

"No," Zeke said again. "Spider-Man locked his *main enemy* in jail."

"Did you flush the ultrasound picture of the baby down the toilet?"

Sophie and Lacie stared at each other. Lacie looked as surprised by that one as Sophie felt.

"Spider-Man did that too," Zeke said. "He had to."

"Why?" Daddy said.

"I don't want to talk about that," Zeke said.

"Does Spider-Man want to talk about it?" Daddy said. "Because Spider-Man's dad does."

Sophie was even more surprised by that.

Daddy's voice got softer. "So what's the problem, superhero?"

Zeke launched into a long explanation of Spider-Man's latest attempt to save somebody from something. Lacie nudged Sophie with a bag of pretzels.

"He gets that from you," she whispered. "You used to blame everything you did wrong on your imaginary characters."

"Only Daddy never believed me," Sophie whispered back.

"Well, go figure," Lacie said.

"Why are we in here whispering anyway?" Sophie said.

"Because I've already figured out why Z-Boy's been behaving like the Tasmanian Devil, and if Dad starts to punish him, I'm stepping in."

The only sound coming from the direction of the snack bar now was the thump of Zeke's tennis shoes as he swung his legs.

"Let me ask you this, Spider-Man," Daddy said. "Do you think there's a new invader coming in? Somebody that people might listen to more than they do you?"

"There you go, Dad," Lacie murmured.

"There *is* gonna be one," Zeke said. "And I don't want it 'cause everybody's already forgetting about me."

The tears in his voice made Sophie want to cry too.

"Then I think Spider-Man's mom and dad need to make sure he knows he'll never be replaced," Daddy said. "What do you say we go upstairs and get to work on that?"

"Is Spider-Man gonna get a punishment?"

"Not if I have anything to do with it," Lacie muttered.

"I'm with ya," Sophie muttered back.

"You two mother hens in the pantry can relax," Daddy said as his voice and Zeke's faded out of the kitchen. "Spider-Man's safe with me."

Lacie grinned. "You rock, Dad," she called to him.

When Sophie got up to her room, she pulled the gauzy curtains closed around her bed and settled against the pillows. As soon as she shut her eyes, she could imagine Jesus. But it was Dr. Peter's voice she heard.

"I don't think any kid is just naturally mean," he'd said. *"Usually a girl acts mean because she's angry or scared. "*

Sophie's eyes came open. Wasn't that what Daddy had just figured out about Zeke? That he was acting like the Terminator because he was afraid everybody would pay more attention to the new baby than him?

So was Phoebe afraid of something? Or somebody?

I'd be afraid of Mr. Karnes if he was my dad, Sophie thought.

But it still didn't make sense that Phoebe would take it out on Maggie.

What else had Dr. Peter said?

Sophie stopped a minute to remember that she was supposed to be mad at Dr. Peter. But she snorted right out loud.

When had he ever told her the wrong thing? She closed her eyes and remembered.

"If Maggie is having trouble with it, you need to bring in some grown-ups."

"We have to," Sophie said out loud. "No matter what we said the plan was before."

In fact, it seemed like every part of their plan was just like Dr. Peter had said: not the right thing to do. They weren't helping Maggie stand up for herself. They were just protecting her, and they weren't even doing it the way Dr. Peter expected — the way the Corn Flakes always do — with honesty and respect and all that good Code stuff. Not when they planned to sneak rehearsals without Phoebe.

And they sure weren't helping Phoebe understand that some of the things she did were heinous. They were just shutting her out.

Down the hall, Zeke giggled in that insane little-boy way. Sophie didn't see how anybody could laugh that hard and not barf.

I guess they convinced him he isn't being replaced by New Baby, Sophie thought.

Sophie tried to get a picture in her mind of Phoebe's skinny, gap-toothed father explaining something to her the way Daddy had talked to Zeke that day, but even she couldn't imagine that. All she could imagine him saying was that all Cubans were good for was hijacking planes and mooching off people.

"Think of Phoebe as a lost lamb instead of a bossy girl who doesn't like Cuban people. Isn't that what Jesus was trying to tell the Pharisees in that story?"

Sophie grabbed her Bible off the night table where it rested in the light of her princess lamp. Luke 15 —

With the bed curtains draped around her like a learned man's robe, Sophie sank herself in. As she read, she saw the kind eyes and heard the voice in the verses.

"Suppose one of you has a hundred sheep and loses one of them."

"I'd leave the rest and go look for it and bring it back," Sophie/the Pharisee said.

That was just what the man named Jesus was saying. *"Then he calls his friends and neighbors together and says, 'Rejoice with me.'"*

I would do that, Sophie/the Pharisee thought. She closed the Bible on her finger. *What I wouldn't do is decide the lamb was just heinous and say, "Serves you right for being so evil."*

Especially if the lost sheep just did it to get attention because it was scared.

"But sometimes a little Pharisee-itis can sneak in—"

"Then it can just sneak right back out," Sophie said out loud. "Right along with our plan."

She scrambled off the bed and headed for the phone in the kitchen, already planning what to say to each of the Corn Flakes. What she *didn't* plan was how to answer Fiona's arguing, Willoughby's skittish little yip, and Darbie's stubborn Irish silence. She finally said they all had a case of Pharisee-itis. Nobody seemed to get it.

Maggie was the hardest one of all.

"I'll just take an F on the project then," she said.

"You don't have to," Sophie said. "We just have to come up with a different plan."

"What if she's still mean to me? I don't want to do this anymore."

Sophie wished Dr. Peter were there to help Maggie get it. She wished she really was Liberty Lawhead so the right words would fall from her lips like silk.

But she knew none of that would happen. The only thing making her try to convince Maggie were the kind eyes—

"Mags?" Sophie said suddenly.

"Yeah."

"Have you talked to Jesus about this, the way Dr. Peter says to?"

"It didn't work. Phoebe's still mean."

Sophie would have made Dr. Peter king of the Corn Flakes if he'd been there, just for giving her the silken words she'd been wishing for.

"Just because it doesn't look like it's working doesn't mean it isn't," she said. "We're not gonna, like, make Phoebe a member of the Corn Flakes. But we did say we'd work with her on this project."

"I didn't know it would be this bad." Maggie's words thudded right through the phone.

"It doesn't have to be." Sophie closed her eyes as she said the rest, just to be sure Jesus' eyes were still there. "We have a Good Shepherd, Mags. We're not lost. We'll be okay after this. But Phoebe doesn't have one."

"I thought only God could save her."

"But we can at least show her that we're not Pharisees."

There was a silence so long Sophie was afraid Maggie had put down the phone and walked off. But finally, some words plunked down.

"I hope Jesus gives you a different plan before Monday," Maggie said.

I hope he does too, Sophie thought as she hung up the phone.

And then she did more than hope. She prayed—long and hard, with her chin in her hands on the snack bar and her eyes squeezed tight. When she opened them, Mama and Daddy were standing there.

"That was some pretty serious daydreaming," Daddy said, roughing up her fuzz with his hand.

"I was praying," Sophie said. "And it was serious. I've got a major problem."

The minute it was out of her mouth, Sophie shook her head. "I'm sorry. I'm not supposed to get you upset, Mama."

"Stop right there." Mama tried to get up on the stool next to Sophie's, and Daddy gave her a boost. "I'm pregnant, but that doesn't make me a piece of glass everybody has to tiptoe around. I want to know what's going on with you."

"And we always will," Daddy said. "No matter how many kids we have."

Sophie looked into their eyes that were almost as kind as the ones she'd seen in her mind. Suddenly, she wanted to cry.

"Okay, dish, Soph," Daddy said. "Are you worried about this baby taking over too?"

Sophie swallowed down a guilty lump. "I haven't even hardly thought about the baby!" she said. "I've been too busy being a Pharisee!"

Daddy pulled up a third stool. "I think I'll sit down for this one."

Sophie told them everything, including the Corn Flakes' plan and how she needed a new one.

"You've come to the right place," Daddy said. "Your mother and I are in planning mode. We just came up with a killer one for dealing with Z-Boy."

"Let us help you," Mama said.

So Sophie did. And when they were done, she felt like Liberty Lawhead herself, chin raised, shoulders straightened—

Except that Liberty Lawhead didn't have a mom who sat with her on the couch and let her feel her tummy until the baby inside fluttered against her hand.

"That's your little sister," Mama said. "We found out today."

"A girl?" Sophie said.

"A little Corn Flake," Mama said.

And for the first time, that tiny flutter of a baby seemed real.

Part of the plan Mama and Daddy helped Sophie form was for her simply to hang with the family over the weekend and let the other Corn Flakes talk to God themselves. They watched movies and took turns feeling for baby moves and played endless games of Chutes and Ladders with Zeke. Since he didn't stuff any of the game pieces up his nose or scream that the whole world was cheating, Sophie actually got into it.

But on Sunday at church, Sophie wasn't sure any of the Corn Flakes had spoken even the first word to God. Willoughby wouldn't look at her. Darbie and Fiona chattered about everything except what they really needed to talk about. Maggie didn't say anything.

"I have a plan," Sophie said.

"So did we," Fiona said. "And I personally think we should stay with it."

"At least let her tell us what it is," Darbie said.

Fiona grunted and gave Sophie a jerky nod.

Sophie told them what she and Mama and Daddy had come up with. "It's way more like a Corn Flake thing than our other plan," she said at the end.

"What if Phoebe just wants to get revenge then?" Willoughby said.

"It could make things worse," Darbie said.

"I hate when we have to do it the right way," Fiona said. "My rotten selfish way is always so much easier."

Darbie sighed. "All right, let's stop foostering about. Pinkie promise."

They locked pinkies. All except Maggie. She left to go to the bathroom.

Sophie tried not to think about that the next morning before school, when Phase One of the Plan went into motion. She went to Mrs. Clayton and told her all about Phoebe and how she thought she needed Round Table help.

As soon as Mrs. Clayton heard Phoebe's name, she shuffled through some file folders on her desk. "Phoebe Karnes," she said. "That's interesting, because she's already on our schedule. Coach Nanini said she has some anger issues he thinks we should work with."

Sophie tried to stay businesslike and not grin too big. Now that Coach Virile was with them, it was hard not to giggle right out loud.

Phase Two was getting through PE with Phoebe. Although they still claimed Sophie was nuts, the Corn Flakes agreed to think of Phoebe as a lost sheep.

"Did you get busted for going after Eddie last Friday?" Fiona asked Phoebe when they were in line for roll call.

Sophie bulged her eyes at Fiona.

"That's Fiona being interested," Darbie whispered.

"Not yet," Phoebe said. "I'm supposed to talk to Mr. Unibrow this period, though. I figure he'll just give me a lecture."

Coach did call Phoebe aside. That meant the Flakes wouldn't do anything until Phase Three, their lunchtime filming session. They were ready for that.

According to the Plan, they met on the school steps, the closest thing they had to a courthouse. Sophie and Maggie went to Mr. Stires' room to get the camera. Mr. Stires was still puttering around with test tubes when they arrived.

"Are you coming out to the filming?" Sophie said.

He chuckled. "Wouldn't miss it. I was just waiting for you girls."

"I don't think we're gonna be filming today," Maggie said from the storage room doorway.

"Why not?" Sophie said. "Mags, don't give up now—"

"No," Maggie said. "Your camera's gone."

Eleven

❀ ✿ ✿

"What do you mean it's gone?" Sophie said. Her voice squeaked beyond itself.

"I mean it's not there," Maggie said. "I looked everywhere."

If Maggie said it wasn't there, it wasn't there, but Sophie had to double-check anyway. She could almost hear Daddy lecturing her as she stared at the empty place on the shelf.

"Nobody else came and got it?" Sophie said to Mr. Stires.

He shook his bald head. His usually happy mustache drooped. "I don't let anybody check it in and out but you."

"Hel-lo-o," Phoebe said from the doorway. "What's taking so long?"

Fiona ran into the back of her. "I told her we were supposed to wait for you out there," she said to Sophie, "but no-o-o, she had to—"

"The camera's gone," Maggie said.

Fiona stared. So did the rest of the group who were now clumped in the doorway.

"You mean, like, stolen?" Willoughby said.

"Let's not jump to conclusions," Mr. Stires said.

But Sophie could see by the faces of the Charms and Flakes that they had already made that leap. Fiona had obviously

100

made another one too, because she was driving her eyes into Phoebe. Phoebe herself was fingering her tooth-gap and staring at Maggie.

"All right, folks." Mr. Stires brushed his fingers back and forth across his mustache about six times. "Let's fan out and look and make sure it didn't just get moved."

"Yeah," Phoebe muttered, "moved to somebody's locker."

They searched Mr. Stires' classroom and storage area until the end of lunch period, but there was no trace of the camera. Vincent even got a magnifying glass out of his backpack and looked for a stray hair they could use for a DNA sample. Jimmy told him he watched too much TV.

When Miss Imes arrived and got the news, her eyebrows shot almost into her scalp. Sophie had to admit Phoebe was probably right. Somebody had stolen her camera.

Jimmy folded his arms and looked shyly at Sophie. "I'm really sorry this happened," he said.

"Yeah, bummer," Nathan said.

Willoughby ran her hand up and down Sophie's back. "Why would somebody do this?"

"Because they're heinous," Fiona said.

"Because they're eejits," Darbie said.

Miss Imes shot silence through them with her eyebrows. "Here's how we'll handle this," she said. "Next period I'm going to make an intercom announcement that the camera has gone missing. I'll ask that it be returned to its original place, no questions asked."

"Then we can check it for fingerprints," Vincent said. "I know how to do that."

"Of course you do," Miss Imes said, "but 'no questions asked' means exactly that. We'll give our thief a chance to reconsider and make this right."

"Not gonna happen," Phoebe said. She gave Maggie one last long look before she exited with a wave of her hand.

She thinks Maggie took it, Sophie thought. *She so does!*

The back of her neck started to prickle—but she closed her eyes and recited the phases in her head.

1. *Tell a grown-up.*
2. *Remember that Phoebe is a scared lost lamb without a shepherd.*
3. *Help Maggie stand up for herself with all the good Corn Flake stuff.*

That second one was harder than ever at the moment, but Sophie made herself pray for Phoebe like the Flakes had all promised to do. That phase of the Plan was supposed to go on all day.

When the bell for fifth period rang and she opened her eyes, there was a note on her desk, folded Fiona-fashion, like a bird.

What about the Plan now? she'd written.

Before Sophie could get her gel pen out to answer, the speaker box squawked. Miss Imes made her announcement, and the class immediately buzzed like a hive.

"I can tell you exactly who did it," Julia said.

"Who?" Colton said. His stick-out ears suddenly reminded Sophie of antennae.

Julia cupped her hands around her mouth. Both Colton and Tod leaned so far into the aisle, Sophie was sure they'd end up in Julia's lap. Sophie had to force herself not to lean too, because she couldn't see what Julia was mouthing.

"Who's Fee-Bee?" Colton said, stretching his lips across his teeth.

"That girl who buys her clothes at Kmart," Anne-Stuart said with the usual sniff. "You know—" She put her finger up to her two front teeth.

Tod's face came to a point at his nose. "You mean that chick that tried to slash Eddie's face with her fingernails?"

Sophie felt her eyes widen, and she turned to Fiona, who was already nodding.

The minute Mr. Stires told the class to pick up their materials for the lab, Sophie got to Fiona with the words already on her lips. "You think Phoebe—"

"I *know* she did—"

"That doesn't make sense!" Sophie said. "All she wants to *do* is this movie. Why would she take the—"

"So she can blame it on Maggie," Fiona said. "Didn't you see the way she looked at her?"

Sophie had; she couldn't deny that.

"*Or*—and you don't know this yet—" Fiona took two test tubes from the tray and pulled Sophie toward their lab station, glancing warily over her shoulder. "When we were all out on the steps waiting for you and Maggie to show up with the camera?"

"Yeah?"

"Phoebe said Coach Nanini told her that she was going to Round Table tomorrow. She said if she got detention and couldn't work on the movie, somebody was going to pay." Fiona grabbed two vials of liquid from the tray Gill was passing by with and lowered her voice. "I'm thinking that somebody is you."

"I still don't get it—"

"If we don't have the camera, we can't keep working on the film without her."

Sophie began to nod. "This film or any other film. We have to tell Miss Imes what we suspect."

Fiona wiggled her eyebrows. "Unless we can prove it ourselves—"

"Un-uh," Sophie said. "We have to do it the right way, or we're just—"

"Yeah, yeah, Pharisees." Fiona flipped open the lab workbook and cut her eyes toward Sophie. "You think she did it, though; I can tell."

Sophie didn't answer, but Fiona kept looking at her.

"Okay," Sophie said finally. "But we have to let the Round Table handle it. And we can't tell Phoebe we think she's guilty."

Fiona bunched up her lips. "I'm gonna have to put duct tape on my mouth."

"After you tell everybody else in the group to keep quiet about it," Sophie said. "Right after class, I'm going to Coach Nanini."

At the end of the period, Sophie raced to Life Skills for a pass from Coach Yates. "Just don't make a career out of it, LaCroix," she said. "I want you back here in fifteen."

Sophie shifted into high gear as she raced down the hall, but at the corner, bony fingers wrapped themselves around her arm. Phoebe hauled her into the girls' restroom.

"I don't have time for this!" Sophie said. "I have to—"

The door slapped closed behind them. Phoebe's mouth came so close to Sophie's face, Sophie thought she might fall right into the gap between her teeth. Phoebe took a step forward, and Sophie backed into a sink.

"Everybody thinks I stole your camera," Phoebe said.

"Who's 'everybody'?" Sophie managed to say. Her voice couldn't have sounded less like Ms. Hess or Liberty Lawhead or anybody else who wasn't squeaking off the scale.

"Those rich chicks with the manicures," Phoebe said. "I heard them running their mouths about me in the hall between fifth and sixth. I get to sixth period and everybody's looking at me like I'm a serial killer or something."

Sophie could only stare. It always amazed her how fast the Corn Pops worked.

"So I gotta ask you something." Phoebe raked her bangs out of her eyes with her fingers. "Do *you* think I did it?"

Sophie opened her mouth, but a tangle of words caught in her throat, and nothing came out.

Phoebe's eyes searched Sophie's face. "You do," she said. "You don't even have to say it—I can see."

Phoebe's lip curled, but not into a smile. She took two steps backward before she turned and headed straight for the door. When she got there, she stopped and looked over her shoulder at Sophie through her fence of bangs.

"I just thought you were better than most people." She made a dramatic exit. But Sophie knew that, for once, Phoebe wasn't acting.

Sophie wasn't sure how long she stood there, arms wrapped around herself, remembering the look on Phoebe's face and feeling the cold of the sink through her parachute pants. Two things were for sure. She now knew what a lost lamb looked like. And she knew what a Pharisee felt like.

Sophie stuffed Coach Yates' pass into the pocket of her hoodie and headed for the door. She'd probably used up ten of her fifteen minutes, but now she had to see Coach Virile more than ever.

He was in the gym, watching lines of eighth-grade boys dribble basketballs up and down the court. The squeal of sneakers was deafening. There were so many long arms and legs dangling between her and Coach Virile, Sophie didn't see who stood next to him until she was almost on them.

It was Phoebe.

Sophie's own sneakers squealed as she stopped dead. But Coach Virile's eyes met hers, and he said something to Phoebe that sent her out onto the court, picking up balls. Coach blew his whistle, and the boys bounded to the bleachers and ran up them, two rows at a time. Coach motioned Sophie toward himself, but now she wasn't sure she wanted to go. There was no guessing what Phoebe had told him. The worst would be if she had told him the truth.

"Hey, Little Bit," he said. "You look like a whupped puppy."

She could hardly hear him over the pounding of feet, but at least she didn't see disappointment in his eyes.

Tell a grown-up, she could hear herself saying to the Flakes.

So she did—all their suspicions and their reasons and her feeling at that moment like a finger-pointing tattletale.

"I had to tell a grown-up that she was being mean to Maggie and scaring her," Sophie said. "And I guess she just wanted to get back at me." She swallowed hard. "Only, how come I feel like maybe she didn't do it?"

"Because maybe she didn't."

He nodded his shiny head toward the court, where Phoebe dragged a bag of basketballs twice her size toward a storage closet. She was bent over like an old woman walking in the wind. Sophie felt a pang inside.

"You don't think she did?" Sophie said.

"She was with me all third period. She's in my fourth-period Life Skills class, and we were talking until the last bell rang for lunch. I'm not a detective, but I don't see where she ever had the chance." He looked down at Sophie, his one big eyebrow hooding his eyes like a visor. "Proving her innocence isn't what's hard for Phoebe right now," he said. "It's dealing with the fact that you automatically assumed she was guilty."

"She automatically assumed Maggie was guilty!"

As soon as she said it, Sophie looked at the floor. "That doesn't make it right, does it?" she said. "I feel like a heinous Pharisee."

"Little Bit."

Sophie looked up. His eyes were kind.

"Why don't you just tell her that?" he said. A smile twitched at his lips. "Only I don't think she knows what a Pharisee is. You might want to change that part."

Sophie felt Phoebe getting closer. When she stopped next to Coach Virile, he pointed to the bottom row of bleachers. They both sat. Coach Virile climbed up to the row behind them and leaned back, arms stretched out.

"I'm here if you need me," he said.

Need you? Sophie wanted to cry. *Do this* for *me!*

Phoebe struck a pose like the victims of kidnapping Sophie had seen on the news, all shaken and brave. Phoebe's eyes watered, and as her lips headed toward a curl, they trembled. Suddenly, it hurt to see her.

"I'm sorry!" Sophie blurted out. "We shouldn't have suspected you right away—I should have thought about you being a lost sheep—only we were mad at you for being prejudiced against Maggie—only we should have done something sooner—only I was being a Pharisee, and I know you don't know what that means, but it's like so heinous and even being nice to you didn't change the way you treated Maggie—and I know we didn't try that hard—"

"Little Bit," Coach Virile said, "take a breath."

Sophie tried, but it was hard. Her chest was squeezing in.

"I didn't steal the camera," Phoebe said.

"I know," Sophie said.

Phoebe looked at Coach Virile. "Then are we done?"

"Are we?" Coach Virile said.

For a second, Sophie was confused as Phoebe shook her head and shoved her bangs back. And then Phoebe said, "I don't know why I act like that to Cuban Girl—"

"Excuse me?" Coach Virile said.

"Maggie," Phoebe said. Her bangs fell in her eyes again, and this time she hid behind them. "She just makes me feel scared. It's like, she's not like regular people, and that freaks me out." Her eyes filled up again. "I don't know why. But he—" She jerked her head toward Coach Nanini. "He's gonna help me figure it out—him and that Round Table thing."

Finally, she looked at Sophie, cringing as if Sophie might slug her.

"I know you hate me," she said, "but don't let them give me detention, okay? I want to do this movie really bad—and I don't want you guys to get a bad grade—and my dad will—"

It was as if her voice caught on something in her throat, and the words stuck. Sophie wasn't sure she could stand to hear them anyway. Not if they matched the fear on Phoebe's face.

The bell rang, sounding far away, as if it belonged to some other school. But with a start, Sophie remembered Coach Yates.

"I was supposed to be back to class in fifteen minutes!" she said.

"I've got your back." Coach Nanini turned to Phoebe. "You have something you want to say to your film buddies?"

Phoebe looked like she would rather have climbed into the bag with the basketballs, but she nodded. Then there was a silence, the kind where no one knows what to say.

Liberty Lawhead would know exactly what to do right now, Sophie thought.

It was the first time she'd thought about Liberty all day. But come to think of it, she, her Sophie-self, did know what to do.

"I'll walk with you," she said to Phoebe.

Coach Nanini made a soft sound in his throat.

"You don't have to," Phoebe said.

"I know," Sophie said.

Phoebe shrugged, slung her backpack over her shoulder, and looked at Coach Nanini with questions in her eyes.

"Come see me when you're done," he said.

Sophie started across the gym, and Phoebe caught up. "I have to go to my locker first," she said.

"I'll go with you," Sophie said.

They dodged the after-school crowd in silence until they were almost to the lockers. Then Phoebe said, "What did you mean when you said I was a lost sheep?" She curled up a smile. "I've been called a lot of things before, but never that."

Sophie stopped beside the locker as Phoebe twirled the combination lock. The Corn Flakes hadn't planned this part. She closed her eyes for a second.

"Hello, what's the deal? Why won't you open?" Phoebe tugged at her locker door. "I hate these things." She started dialing again. "Are you going to tell me why I'm a sheep or not?"

"It's from the Bible," Sophie said.

"I'm in the Bible?" Phoebe said, frowning at her lock. "Go figure."

"We all are," Sophie said.

"You're a sheep too?" Phoebe said.

"Yeah. Only I'm not lost. You know, because of Jesus."

"Is that what you talk about in that class you go to?" Phoebe gave the locker door a yank, and it flew open, knocking her back a step. She stared into the locker. Sophie stared with her.

Because there, inside, was Sophie's camera.

Twelve

I don't know how it got there, I swear!" Phoebe said.

Her face went as white as teeth. Sophie could feel the color draining out of hers too. All she could do was gape at her camera, displayed like a museum piece on top of Phoebe's books.

"Here she is!" she heard Willoughby say behind her.

Those were the last clear words Sophie understood for a while. The rest was all gasps and people coming and going in scenes.

Miss Imes appeared and took Phoebe to the office with the camera.

Mrs. Clayton came and said there would be a Round Table meeting the next day at lunch.

The Corn Pops arrived in a bunch and told each other out of the sides of their glossy mouths that they always knew Phoebe was nothing but trash. Fruit Loops stuck in words like "Dude!" and "Sweet" and "Score," none of which seemed to fit at all.

Several teachers finally herded the gathering crowd outside to get on their buses.

Through it all, Sophie's thoughts circled in her brain.

I was almost sure she didn't do it. But my camera was in her locker.

Coach Virile says she couldn't have done it.

But how did it get in her locker if she didn't put it there?

"She's just a lost lamb with a mean father," Sophie said out loud. "Right?"

She blinked. Fiona, Maggie, and Darbie stood on the sidewalk, staring at her.

"That doesn't make it okay for her to commit grand larceny," Fiona said.

Sophie shook her head. "She didn't."

"Sophie," Darbie said, "the bloomin' camera was sitting right in her locker."

"Somebody else must have put it there," Sophie said.

"Why are you defending her?" Fiona glanced over at Maggie. "After all the stuff she's done."

"But she didn't do *this*," Sophie said. And then she told them what Coach Virile had said, and how Phoebe had looked, and how that had felt. By the time she was finished, her bus had pulled up and kids were boarding.

Fiona groaned. "I guess you're not going to let us off and leave it to the Round Table to handle this, are you?" she said.

"No," Sophie said. "Somebody planted my camera in her locker, and we have to prove it before the Round Table meets."

"Tell me again why we're going to all this trouble for that little blackguard?" Darbie said.

"Because she doesn't have anybody else to do it for her," Sophie said. "We all have each other—and we have Dr. Peter—and we have Jesus. Phoebe's just—lost."

Nobody shook her head or groaned or whined. Fiona just said, "I hate it when you're right."

"Hurry, she's closing the door," Darbie said, pushing Sophie gently up the bus steps.

Sophie stopped at the top and looked back at Maggie, who hadn't said a word. "Are you going to help, Mags?" Sophie said.

Maggie didn't answer. Sophie sagged.

"In or out, missy?" the bus driver said.

Sophie stepped inside and watched through the closed doors as Maggie turned away and went to her own bus. Sophie flopped into a seat and leaned against her lump of a backpack, now softer without her camera inside. Everything seemed to sink.

What was Daddy going to say when she told him? And how were they going to find out who planted the camera by lunchtime tomorrow?

And what about Maggie? How was she going to deal with all this?

Liberty Lawhead leaned across the backseat of the limo and brought her face close. "The same way you always do. A great civil rights leader listens to the counsel of her advisers—especially to the greatest leader, who lives in her heart and bestows his kind eyes on her. Then she waits, and she knows, and she follows. She isn't lost, because she knows her Shepherd."

Sophie opened her eyes and rubbed the crop of fuzz on her head. *I never heard Liberty Lawhead talk like that*, she thought. *I didn't know she knew that much about Jesus.*

And then she smiled at herself in the glass. Of course. Liberty Lawhead knew, because *she* knew.

But that didn't mean everything was easy after that.

When Sophie told Mama and Daddy about the camera, Daddy got his halftime-in-the-locker-room face on. It took Sophie half an hour to convince him that Phoebe wasn't guilty. Then Mama got her somebody's-going-to-get-hurt-on-the-field look on, and it took Sophie another thirty minutes to assure her that the Flakes and the Charms wouldn't be in danger looking for the real culprit. She had to promise to tell Mama and Daddy and a grown-up from the Round Table what they planned to do before they started.

The next hardest thing was coordinating the Flakes and the Charms. Sophie received so many e-mails that night, Daddy finally turned the computer completely over to her. In her final Instant Message exchange with Fiona, it was decided that the Charms would find out all the ways somebody could get into someone else's locker and investigate.

WordGirl: Vincent is all over that.
DreamGirl: Ya think?
WordGirl: LOL
WordGirl: Willoughby will check out the rumor situa-
            tion and do squelching duty.
DreamGirl: U and Darbie work on Mags.
WordGirl: Thanks for giving us the hardest job.
DreamGirl: I have the hardest job.
WordGirl: Phoebe?
DreamGirl: You know it.

As she lay in bed imagining Jesus, though, Sophie knew how she'd handle Phoebe. The only way there was to handle a lost sheep.

But it still didn't get easier after that. The only Round Table adult they could find to tell about their investigation plans before school was Mrs. Clayton. She tapped her blonde helmet with a red pen and looked at them with her blue-bullet eyes.

"I appreciate your trying to help this girl," she said. "That is, after all, what the Round Table is about. But the evidence is fairly clear. Today's meeting is more about helping Phoebe change than determining her guilt or innocence."

"So she won't actually get in trouble?" Fiona said.

Mrs. Clayton bulleted her eyes again. "There will be consequences for the theft. That's a serious thing."

"Not as serious as what her father's going to do to her," Sophie said when they were out in the hall.

"Then we better get started," Jimmy said.

But Phoebe wasn't in third-period PE class, and Coach Yates wasn't in the mood for answering questions. It was all she could do to break up the gossip groups just so she could take roll. Maggie was there, but she stayed away from the Flakes. Willoughby reported that she hadn't said a word all through first and second periods. The same was definitely *not* true of the two Corn Pops in her classes, B.J. and Cassie.

"All they could talk about," Willoughby said, "was how Phoebe is white trash, and she's gonna be put in Juvie Hall, and the Round Table is gonna be broken up because it isn't doing any good—"

"No way." Fiona parked a ball on her hip.

"It isn't working on Eddie." Willoughby gave a nervous poodle-yip, and her eyes went wide. "He was all talking about how Phoebe was like this criminal because she attacked him—and he was bragging about how if Coach Nanini hadn't been there, he would have taken Phoebe out."

"I'm impressed," Darbie said in a dry voice. "Big blaggard like that taking out a skinny little thing like Phoebe."

"Yeah," Willoughby said, yipping more happily. "What a man."

"Speaking of men—" Fiona pointed at Nathan, who was jogging toward them from across the gym.

Sophie could tell by the neon pink of his ears that he was going to talk to them.

But instead, he tripped a few feet away. In the process of untangling his legs, he pulled a piece of paper out of his sneaker and kicked it toward Sophie. She picked it up as he flailed away.

Sophie stared at the writing scrawled across the paper. "Listen. 'CSI has detected suspicious markings on alleged thief's locker, indicating forced entry with a metal object. Fresh shavings indicate this was recent activity. We have a digital photo. Investigation continues to identify said object.'"

"What?" Willoughby said. "Why can't he speak English?"

"Somebody opened Phoebe's locker with something metal!" Fiona said.

"Hi, Mags!" Darbie said.

Sophie turned around to see Maggie standing just a few feet from her. But before she could say a word, Maggie's eyes flashed, and she hurried away.

A blast from Coach Yates' whistle bounced off the gym walls. "Let's go, people! I'm in the mood to give detentions!"

The Corn Flakes latched onto each other and sprinted for the drill line. Sophie looked over her shoulder, but she couldn't find Maggie.

"She's our job," Darbie said.

"Yours is to find Phoebe and tell her there's hope," Fiona said.

Sophie liked hearing the tone in Fiona's voice, as if she were really pulling for Phoebe. But she wasn't sure how much hope she could give the lost lamb.

She crumpled the note and stuck it in the waistband of her track pants. *This doesn't really prove anything,* she thought. *Not unless somebody was seen doing it.*

And even if somebody had, the chances of him coming forward got slimmer by the minute. The gym, the locker room, the halls between classes throbbed with talk of Phoebe the Thief. It seemed like the entire student body of GMMS was ready to hang her from the flagpole.

If they could only find her.

Fourth period was almost over, and Sophie still hadn't had a chance to talk to her. When the bell rang for lunch, she practically ran to the Round Table meeting room. Maybe the office had been keeping her, Sophie thought, and they would bring her in before the meeting started.

But the only person there was Jimmy, holding out a digital camera to Sophie. His shy face told her their ongoing investigation had turned up nothing.

"The pictures of the locker are on here," he said.

"Thanks," Sophie said. "But I don't think they'll do any good."

"It'll create reasonable doubt." Jimmy shrugged his gymnast-shoulders. "I think I watch too much TV too."

"Is that like, if there's any doubt at all, they can't say she stole it?" Sophie said.

"Yeah," Jimmy said.

Sophie watched as the eighth graders trailed in whispering to each other, and Mrs. Clayton talked into Coach Nanini's ear just inside the doorway.

"I don't know," Sophie said to Jimmy. "It's like everybody's already made up their minds, just because she's poor or something."

"It's discrimination," Jimmy said.

Sophie felt her mouth falling open. "It *is*, huh?"

"It's like Phoebe's a Marielito now—"

"And everybody thinks she'd steal just because she looks like people who do!" Sophie lowered her voice. "Do you think I can convince them?"

"Are you serious?" Jimmy whispered back. "I don't think there's anybody else who could."

Sophie decided that was the thing she liked about him best, best, *best* of all.

But she was still shaky inside when Mrs. Clayton called the meeting to order and explained Phoebe's case.

"So why are we here?" Hannah the eighth grader said, blinking away at her contact lenses.

Oliver slouched down in his chair, gesturing with one hand. "She should just go to Juvie for this. If she's already heisting people's stuff, how are we supposed to change her?"

"We can't change people," Sophie said. "We just have to see who they really are."

"She showed us who she is," Oliver said.

But Coach Nanini put up his hand and nodded at Mrs. Clayton, who slipped out of the room. Sophie's heart sank. Mrs. Clayton was one of the people who needed to hear this.

"Go ahead, Little Bit," Coach Nanini said.

Liberty Lawhead lifted her chin. She had to say what she had to say, whether anyone believed her or not —

And then Sophie LaCroix lifted *her* chin and said, "Phoebe didn't have a chance to steal the camera. Coach Nanini can testify to that. And she wouldn't have anyway, because without the camera we can't make the movie, and she *lives* to make movies because she has such an awful home life. And I don't know what she'd do with it because all she wants to do is act — she doesn't even know how to turn the camera on."

"Then how did it get in her locker?" Oliver said.

Sophie looked at Jimmy, who produced the digital camera. "We have evidence that somebody might have gotten Phoebe's locker open with some kind of metal thing."

"Let's see," Hannah said.

Jimmy handed the camera to her. Oliver craned his neck to see.

"Still doesn't prove somebody framed her," he said.

"But it gives—" Sophie groped for the words.

"Reasonable doubt," Jimmy said.

Hannah looked up from the camera. "I don't see why we should give her the benefit of the doubt. She attacked Eddie Wornom right in front of Coach Nanini. And I don't mean to be snotty or anything, but she isn't exactly an honor student—"

"Phoebe," Coach Nanini said, "do you have anything to say to that?"

Sophie jerked around to see Phoebe standing near the door with Mrs. Clayton. Her eyes were red-rimmed and swimming.

"I didn't do it," Phoebe said.

Mrs. Clayton nudged Phoebe toward a seat, and Coach Nanini said, "Let's give Phoebe a chance to speak for herself."

"Do you know of anybody who'd want to get you in trouble?" Oliver said.

"Is anybody mad at you?" Hannah said.

Phoebe curled her lip. "Who isn't?"

"I'm not," Sophie said.

"See, I don't get that," Hannah said, eyes blinking double-time. "If it were my camera that got stolen, I'd be so ticked off—"

"Let's stick to the facts," Mrs. Clayton said. "Bottom line: all the evidence points to you, Phoebe. Yes, you'll have to take responsibility for that, but we just want to help you so you won't do something like this again."

"I didn't do it in the first place!" Phoebe said.

There was a knock on the door, and Miss Imes got up. Sophie closed her eyes. The whole conversation was like a wheel spinning and not getting anywhere.

"Just stop," Sophie said.

The room got quiet.

"Go ahead, Little Bit," Coach Nanini said.

"Okay," Sophie said, "Phoebe has an awful father, and she doesn't have any friends, and she acts because she's scared, and I don't know of what, but she is." She took a breath. "Why can't we help her with that and forget about the camera?"

"I wish we could, Sophie," Mrs. Clayton said. "But we can't just let it go." She turned to Phoebe. "It would be so much better for you if you would just admit that you took—"

"I might as well," Phoebe said, lips quivering. "You've already made up your minds—"

"No!" Sophie said.

"Wait," somebody else said.

Miss Imes opened the door wider, and Mr. Janitor Man stepped in. Right behind him was Maggie.

"What's up with that?" Jimmy whispered to Sophie.

The only other person in the room who looked as shocked as Sophie felt was Phoebe. And then Phoebe's whole body began to shake.

"Don't believe anything she says against me!" Phoebe cried out, pointing at Maggie. "You want to know who's mad at me and wants me to get in trouble? It's her! I treated her like dirt, and now she wants to nail me—"

"Hold on," Miss Imes said. "It's nothing like that." She stood behind Maggie and put her hands on Maggie's shoulders. Sophie could see Mags stiffening, and her eyes went straight to Sophie. Then they darted away, as if she were ashamed of something.

NO! Sophie wanted to cry out to her. *Don't tell them you did it. I don't care about the camera—we'll help you. We're all Corn Flakes—*

But Miss Imes was already saying, "Tell them what you know, Maggie," and Maggie was opening her mouth.

Sophie clung to the arm of the chair. Why had Maggie done it? They were getting ready to help her stand up to Phoebe. Why hadn't she trusted the Corn Flakes?

"I have a confession," Maggie said. Her voice was heavy. "I wasn't going to tell anybody because I kind of wanted her to take the blame."

"I told you," Phoebe said.

Mrs. Clayton told her to shush.

"I saw somebody throw a big screwdriver in the trash can by the lockers yesterday," Maggie went on. "Right next to Phoebe's locker."

A big screwdriver—

"And he was looking all around like he didn't want anybody to see him do it, so I hid—"

He?

"And he met this girl in the hall and she said, 'Did you get it in there?' and he went—" Maggie turned a thumb upward.

"Maybe he used the screwdriver to get Phoebe's locker open," Jimmy said.

"Who?" Hannah and Oliver said together.

But Sophie knew, even before Maggie said, "Eddie Wornom." The room came alive.

"Wait a minute now, before we get all excited," Coach Nanini said. "Eddie was using that screwdriver to help me with the bleachers, but I sent him to return it."

Mr. Janitor Man raised a finger. "Never got it," he said in his sandpapery voice. "Me and her" — he glanced at Maggie — "just went through yesterday's trash bags. Found it."

He reached into his tool belt and pulled out the same screwdriver Eddie had thrown at Phoebe.

"Maybe we can get prints," Jimmy muttered to Sophie.

Coach Virile stormed out of the room like a bull charging a fence. Mrs. Clayton was still watching Maggie.

"Who was the girl?" she said.

"B.J. Schneider," Maggie said.

"Do you know her?" Mrs. Clayton said to Phoebe.

Phoebe shook her head, but Sophie was nodding hers.

"B.J. was there the day he" — Sophie nodded toward Mr. Janitor Man — "was fixing Eddie's locker. She saw him get the door open with a screwdriver."

"Mr. Fenwick?" Mrs. Clayton said to the janitor.

He grunted. "I remember. One of them told me that was 'Eddie's locker' like it was King Tut's tomb."

"That actually does sound like B.J.," Mrs. Clayton said. She looked around the room. "But I want all of you to understand that this doesn't prove Eddie planted the camera — "

"Don't need to." Coach Virile stepped into the room and pulled Eddie in after him, lunch ketchup still at the corners of his mouth. "Eddie's going to prove it himself. Let's go, Mr. Wornom."

Eddie turned his radish-red face toward Phoebe. "You're trash," he said. "If I hadn't of gotten caught, they woulda kept thinking you did it."

Beneath the voices that all rose at once, Jimmy's made its way to Sophie. "I guess he proved it," he said.

There was a lot to sort out before the Round Table adjourned that day. Maggie apologized to Phoebe for not coming forward right away. Phoebe apologized to Maggie for being hateful—at least as much as Phoebe could, Sophie decided. Phoebe got Campus Commission with Coach Nanini for attacking Eddie—which brought on a gap-toothed smile. Eddie was taken out of their hands by Mr. Bentley, the principal.

Although it was almost time for fifth period when they left Round Table, the rest of the Corn Flakes and the Lucky Charms were waiting for them in the hall.

"They talked me into telling," Maggie said.

"We saw her with Vincent's note that must have fallen out of your track pants, Soph," Fiona said.

"And she was all bummed out," Willoughby put in.

"So we interrogated her," Fiona said.

"But we were nice," Darbie said. "Corn Flake style."

Fiona grinned. "Just doing our job."

"And we did ours," Vincent said. He pulled a Q-Tip out of his pocket. "If Wornom hadn't confessed, I was ready to get his DNA."

"I guess I'm the only one who didn't do my job," Sophie said. "I never even got to talk to Phoebe."

"She's right there," Fiona said, nodding down the hall.

Phoebe was indeed lounging by the water fountain.

"I don't think she's standing there because she's thirsty, Soph," Darbie said.

Sophie tilted her chin and walked toward the victim of discrimination whose rights she had just stood up for.

I can't change her, she thought in an inner voice that sounded very much like Liberty Lawhead's. *But I can help her see who she really is. Well*, she added as she dodged the last person between her and the Diva at the water fountain, *Jesus and me, that is.*

Glossary

blackguards (bLAK gards) very rude and offensive people

civil rights (siv-il rites) laws and ideas that are supposed to make sure everyone is treated equally. Civil rights movements try to bring attention to people who need these rights.

delusion (di-LOO-shun) believing something is there when it's not, and thinking it's still there no matter what anyone tells you

Dr. Martin Luther King Jr. (Doktor Mar-tin Loo-thur King Joon-yur) a very important man in the 1960s. He used nonviolence to help make African Americans equal in the United States. He was shot and killed on April 4, 1968.

flan (flahn) a really thick and wiggly custard dessert that is popular in some Hispanic cultures

foostering about (FOO-stur-ing a-bout) an Irish way of saying "stop wasting time"

heinous (HEY-nus) unbelievably mean and cruel

illusion (eh-LOO-shun) when something looks incredibly real, but it isn't

Latino (lah-TEE-no) a person whose family was originally from Latin America (Central and South America), but who now lives in the United States

Marielitos (mar-e-el-EE-toes) people who left Cuba by boat to Key West to be free from the Cuban government. They lived in tents on an Air Force base until the U.S. government could find places for them to live, and some people treated them badly afterward because they believed the Marielitos were all criminals.

monologue (MAW-nol-og) a long speech given by one person who doesn't allow anyone else to talk

phlegm (flem) thick, icky stuff in your throat that usually appears when you're sick

scuttlebutt (skuh-tell-but) juicy rumors and gossip

statuesque (stah-chew-ESK) tall and graceful, and looking a lot like a really impressive statue

swordplay (sord-play) showing you can use a sword very well, and could defend yourself if necessary

virile (VEAR-uhl) the definition of manly; muscular, strong, and really hunky. Think cute movie star meets not-icky body-builder.

Sophie Series
Written by Nancy Rue

Meet Sophie LaCroix, a creative soul who's destined to become a great film director someday. But many times, her overactive imagination gets her in trouble!

Book 1: Sophie's World
IBSN: 978-0-310-70756-1

Book 2: Sophie's Secret
ISBN: 978-0-310-70757-8

Book 3: Sophie Under Pressure
ISBN: 978-0-310-71840-6

Book 4: Sophie Steps Up
ISBN: 978-0-310-71841-3

Book 5: Sophie's First Dance
ISBN: 978-0-310-70760-8

Book 6: Sophie's Stormy Summer
ISBN: 978-0-310-70761-5

Available now at your local bookstore!
Visit www.faithgirlz.com, it's the place for girls ages 9-12.

faiThGirLz!
the beauty of believing

Sophie Series
Written by Nancy Rue

Book 7: Sophie's Friendship Fiasco
ISBN: 978-0-310-71842-0

Book 8: Sophie and the New Girl
ISBN: 978-0-310-71843-7

Book 9: Sophie Flakes Out
ISBN: 978-0-310-71024-0

Book 10: Sophie Loves Jimmy
ISBN: 978-0-310-71025-7

Book 11: Sophie's Drama
ISBN: 978-0-310-71844-4

Book 12: Sophie Gets Real
ISBN: 978-0-310-71845-1

Available now at your local bookstore!
Visit www.faithgirlz.com, it's the place for girls ages 9-12.

ZONDERkidz
.com

Bibles

Every girl wants to know she's totally unique and special. This Bible says that with Faithgirlz! sparkle! Now girls can grow closer to God as they discover the journey of a lifetime, in their language, for their world.

The NIV Faithgirlz! Bible

Hardcover
ISBN 978-0-310-71581-8

Softcover
ISBN 978-0-310-71582-5

The NIV Faithgirlz! Bible

Italian Duo-Tone™
ISBN 978-0-310-71583-2

The NIV Faithgirlz! Backpack Bible

Periwinkle
Italian Duo-Tone™
ISBN 978-0-310-71012-7